BREAKING THE GIRL

Also by Kim Corum:

Playtime

99 Martinis

Heartbreaker

BREAKING THE GIRL

a novel

Kim Corum

Writers Club Press
San Jose New York Lincoln Shanghai

Breaking the Girl
a novel

Writers Club Press
an imprint of iUniverse, Inc.

For information address:
iUniverse, Inc.
5220 S. 16th St., Suite 200
Lincoln, NE 68512
www.iuniverse.com

Any resemblance to actual people and events is purely coincidental. This is a work of fiction.

ISBN: 0-595-24057-7

Printed in the United States of America

For Kris
(Thanks for making me always try new things…)

Don't try this at home.

"Please," I said. "Just let me—"

"No," he hissed and pulled my hand away from between my legs. "Not yet."

"Please," I begged. "Please just let me touch it!"

"No," he mumbled, then, "No, Kristine, not until I say!"

That didn't stop me from trying.

The belt cracked against my ass. It drove a ferocious welt into my skin and burned like fire. I moaned.

"Please," I begged. "Please, please, *please*!"

"No."

It's always the same with us. Always the same with me. I always do this. I always beg to get it done and over with before the show has even really begun. I just can't wait. That's my problem. Impatience.

"I can do it this once," I said, my voice rising to fever pitch. "Then I can do it again and—"

"Shh. Be quiet."

I stopped talking, begging, pleading. Plotting. I wasn't going to win him over. It was his way or no way. And I knew that. So it was his way.

He bent down in front of me, taking my head between his hands. I couldn't see him. My eyes were covered by a silk scarf, the one we used on special occasions, like a birthday or an anniversary. We celebrated at least once a week, regardless.

He rubbed my face and kissed me. My mouth opened and welcomed his tongue, sucked on it, loved its soft edges. My tongue drew circles on his, arousing a soft moan from his lips that came from deep down inside. I kissed him, hoping to soften him so he would allow me to touch myself and get the torture over and done with. But he knew what he was doing. He was withholding so the pleasure—the orgasm—would be doubled, tripled even. So it would be so intense I would shake and shiver and moan and groan and dance and sing. And beg for another.

I ground my crotch against the bed, moving my hips up and down. I was *this* close. This close and I needed to do it. Actually, my body just did it on its own; I just followed it and allowed it to search out the spot.

The belt came down hard again, halting me. A scream erupted from my lips. It was one of those I couldn't stop. I wailed until I my throat was dry and my voice cracked. Another whack, another hoarse scream, this time less intense.

He put a gag in my mouth.

This time, I couldn't take it anymore. This time was different from the last. The last time had gone on half the night. The last time we tried this was yesterday. I couldn't wait like I had then. No. No. No! I had to have it now. GIVE IT TO ME!

I couldn't utter a word and charm him into doing what I wanted. I couldn't bat my eyes and make him feel guilty. I was totally helpless. Which is what he liked best.

Then he got behind me and I felt him glide his cock into me. Ahhh! YES! YES! The end was near. I was exhausted. But soon I'd be released. Freed. Unchained. And it'd be worth it, all of it.

As he began to fuck me, he said, "Tomorrow, we're going to try something different."

I cocked my head to the side and listened, hanging on his every word.

"Tomorrow, I'm going to tie you up."

Tie me up, tie me down, beat me, switch me, hold me tight, love me forever.

It never occurred to me to say, *This isn't natural.* Well, it did. Once. And I immediately dismissed the thought.

First of all, just let me say, I wasn't that kind of girl. I didn't like submission or domination and sex was just plain sex and though I had good sex, it never really ever went beyond the meat and potatoes variety. Me on top. Him—whoever he might be at that moment—on top. Cowgirl—facing *and* reverse. I tried anal once and only once and that was enough. (I only did it cause I was drunk and the guy would not leave me alone.) Doggie. The 69. The basic stuff no one actually sat down and taught you but you figured it out on your own. Because, well, it *is* second nature. Sex, I mean.

But to have someone tie me up? No. To have someone blindfold me? Uh uh. That just wasn't my bag. I just wasn't that kind of "tie me up, tie me down, beat me, switch me, hold me tight, love me forever" kind of girl. And if a guy tried to pull any of that shit, I was out the door. Goodbye, asshole. It just wasn't me. I was not that kind of girl.

He was that kind of guy. Which made me that kind of girl.

"You love it," he said once. "You love it when I'm in control of you, when you don't have a choice in what's going to happen to you or to your body. Tell me you love it."

"I love it."

And I did. I won't sit here and deny that. Let me rephrase it, though. *I loved doing it with him.* He was special to me. Special because he knew how to push my buttons, get me going and take me over the edge to that never-never land of multiple orgasm that left me weak, fragile and begging for more.

And I begged. I begged for it all. I wanted it all. Once I started doing it, once I got over that roadblock, there were no boundaries left. No restrictions and certainly no limitations.

And there was no conclusion in sight. All I saw, all I thought of, was him and what he was going to do next. I wasn't a slave. I was a willing participant.

In the end, I knew what he was doing. He was beating me down, taking control of my body, my mind and my soul. Then he'd rebuild it. Brick by brick, using his words of love to re-master me until I stood new in his eyes, in the image he had created for me, of me.

Ain't love a bitch?

        ✦.   ✦   ✦

Maybe I should start at the beginning.

Let me just say that when I first saw him, I didn't see sparks. I didn't have an immediate attraction to him. Sure, he was handsome in that aloof, businessman kind of way. I liked his smile. But it didn't go beyond that. It didn't go beyond because he was a customer and I didn't go there with customers. I was a stripper. In New Orleans.

He kinda reminded me of Gatsby. That's the image I had of him all along. I'd always had a fondness for literary characters and I believed Gatsby to be far and above the best. He was so romantic, yet so vulnerable. Frank was romantic. He was not vulnerable. Obviously, I was. Like Gatsby, he watched from the sidelines before he made his initial move and after he made it, I was hooked.

I hadn't even planned on staying in New Orleans. I had gone to Mardi Gras with my friend, Chelsea. I'd just gotten dumped and was still reeling from the break-up when she offered a temporary solution to my blues: Mardi Gras. She'd even paid the way. She had just divorced her super-rich husband and could afford it. The girl was rolling in dough, which she was hell-bent on spending. She was afraid he'd try to take it back. She said, "If it's not there, he can't get his slimy little paws on it."

Mardi Gras was the best party. I danced with strangers all night long in the French Quarter, flashed my tits for beads, drank way too many hurricanes and threw up in Jackson Square. I loved it. Every bit. That Mardi Gras was one of the best times I've ever had.

On our last night there, we were walking by Tempest, the strip-club. The bouncer in the doorway stopped us and offered us free admittance. Why not? We went in, sat down a few feet from the stage and giggled like schoolgirls. The girl who was onstage got pretty pissed off at us.

She yelled, "If you think you can do better, get your asses up here and do it!"

Never one to back down from a challenge, Chelsea jumped up there, dragging me with her, and proceeded to strip. At first, I was horrified, but then I looked around. The place was packed and all the people in there were egging us on. So Chelsea and I did our "girl/girl" routine we pull on guys in bars (so they'll buy us drinks) and gave everyone a little show. The stripper even joined in. Soon we had our own threesome and after it was over, Chelsea and I were fifty bucks richer.

It was a blast, pure and simple, it was a blast. The manager gave us a free drink and the other strippers sat at our table and began to tell us how much money we could make doing what we'd just done.

It seemed like a good idea at the time. So, yeah. It just kinda worked out like that.

Chelsea and I extended our visit. For two weeks, then she was bored and ready to go back home. But I wasn't, mainly because I was never been one to turn down money. Not that kind of money and I was raking it in. Besides, stripping off my clothes every night made me feel like I had some measure of power. To have the complete undivided attention from those men (and women) gave me a thrill. To know they were hot for me made me feel special. I slowly became the most uninhibited person I knew. And once you do it and get over that hang-up, it's no big deal.

So why not make some money while you're at it?

Chelsea went back home to our little town of Castile, Tennessee and I set up residence in the Quarter with one of the other strippers, Jackie. She and I soon became best friends. We'd leave the club about two in the morning, then hit the clubs, dance till dawn then go out for breakfast, back to the apartment where we'd crash, get up around seven that night, shower and go to it again.

This went on for about six months.

I don't really know what got into me to start acting this way, but for the first time in my life, I was free. I was free. Free to do whatever I wanted. I had no obligations. I was a free agent. I was thirty-two going on nineteen. I'd always done what was expected of me before: Graduate high school, go to college, flunk out, get a menial job, marry my boyfriend, divorce him, go to bars and try to find another one to take his place, fail miserably and wake up with some Neanderthal. The same stuff we all do, rotating our time between work, drink and sex.

Now I was doing what I wanted, when I wanted and was making more money than I could have ever imagined making. I was having the time of my life. I had to lie about my age to get the job. I looked younger than I was and, luckily, my tits still pointed to the ceiling instead of down at the floor. I sure as hell didn't get the job because of my dancing ability.

I never knew my life could change so drastically in such a short span of time. It was like once I let go of the past, and of all the things holding me back, I freed myself to all these different experiences. I not only let go of a shitty job, I let go of a shitty life. And once I let go, everything just opened up.

Then he came into my life. He. Him. Frank.

Once he was there, I could not for the life of me push him away. He stuck to me like super glue and nothing could tear him away. He became a permanent fixture, someone that I could never imagined living without once he was in. And there was no "before" after he came into my life. "Before" disappeared. It disappeared because it didn't matter anymore.

I could stop here and say things like, *Well, if I had called in sick that night, none of this would have happened. If I had gone home when mom called and asked me to, I would have never met him. If I had let one of the other girls give him a private dance, we would have never hooked up.* But he didn't want one of the other girls. He wanted me.

The thing is, I'm not gonna say any of that. I don't regret meeting him. And I don't really regret the things that happened between us. The fact is, I don't regret it. Regrets are for fools. They do nothing but allow people to wallow in their own misery, give a name to the misery and guilt they feel and give it a reason to ruin their lives.

I won't do that. It's not worth it.

Besides, I did enjoy myself. Tremendously. As with the stripping, being involved in a relationship like that is something I could never have imagined for myself. It just wasn't my thing. But once it happened, it just seemed natural, like second nature.

Love can change your mind about all sorts of things and drag your heart along with it, convincing you that there is no way you could ever live without this person who is as sublime as a sunrise and as transcendent as dusk. It can change your mind to include something as subversive as this story I'm going to tell.

His name was Frank.

Just Frank. His last name really doesn't matter. It was Smith or Jones or Gallagher or…Hell. Just pick one. They're really all the same. I didn't know that much about him. I would press him for information that I felt I needed to know, but he'd never tell me anything. He'd say it didn't matter. It did, of course. It did, at first. After a while, no, it didn't matter.

He didn't want to know anything about me. He didn't care to know about my childhood (single parent home), my siblings (one older sister, Caroline, one younger brother, Paul) how I did in school (straight "C" student—I hated it), about my divorce (hellacious—the fucker would just not "let" me go) or why my last boyfriend broke up with me (I asked him to and to my utter surprise and delight, he did). He didn't care that I always cheated in relationships and that's why I couldn't "keep a man", as my mother would say.

The thing is, I never wanted a man, let alone enough to "keep" one and I only cheated to get men out of my life, to drive them away. To me, men were useful on two fronts: 1) To fix shit; and 2) To fuck.

The fact was, I didn't want to be tied down. I was afraid if I was tired down, I'd miss out on something.

Sure, when I'd get dumped (or do the actual dumping) I'd act all heartbroken and eat the obligatory ice cream and do the obligatory soul searching, but within a week, just before the pity I was getting from everyone was about to run out, I'd perk up and move on. So, yeah, I never really attached myself to anyone. Not really. Not until him anyway. And I wanted him with every cell in my body. I wanted him to love me, like I loved him. I don't know if he ever did. He said he did, but who could tell? I think he did, but there was always some measure of doubt hanging around my head.

That's a lie. I knew he loved me. There was never any doubt after the first time he told me.

I never knew I'd want someone so much. So much that he would become my obsession, my force of life. So much that I would—literally—let him walk all over me. And enjoy every second of it.

Private show.

As I've said, I didn't feel an immediate attraction to Frank. He was just another customer who had requested a private show in the backroom. His request would help pay my rent.

I was working a table of college boys (cheap asses) when the manager, Tom, came over and jerked his head to the side. I looked over. And there he was.

"So?" I asked.

"He'd like a private show," he whispered in my ear.

I eyed the man. He looked extremely elegant in his expensive suit. He even had on cufflinks. Gold ones.

"Come on, Kristy," he said and held out his hand.

"Excuse me, boys," I said and smiled at them. "I'll be right back."

Tom led me over to him. I studied him as we approached his table, wondering what was up with him. He studied me as well. His look was more than a little disconcerting. It was plain weird. He looked at me in a way that made me feel strange. As if he didn't own me, but it would only be a matter of time before he would. I didn't like that look. I didn't like it when men assumed I was a cheap whore, even if I did work as a stripper. I didn't like it. I didn't like it one bit.

He was handsome, beyond handsome, really. Old movie star handsome, like Rudolph Valentino handsome. Elegant. He could have stepped out of a silent picture with a highball glass in one hand

and stunningly beautiful woman on the other. And he wouldn't have looked out of place.

His manners were even elegant. The way he smiled, only slightly, as we approached him. The way he cocked his head to the side and drank in my body, which was clad in a tight, aquamarine tank dress. He studied the way my breasts were trying to burst out of the top of my dress. The way my feminine curves jutted this way and that. He seemed especially pleased at my dark hair, which was pulled back into a ponytail. My face perfected with makeup, bringing out the blue in my eyes. My full red lips made even redder by lipstick.

He didn't so much as take me in as suck me in. I don't think he missed anything. He definitely liked what he saw. And as I stared at him, the feeling was mutual. His eyes were this intense shade of blue. They were so blue, they looked fake. I'd never seen eyes like that on anyone.

We stopped in front of him. He smiled—or tried to—up at us and nodded his appreciation.

"Come with us," Tom said and he followed us to the backroom which was so dark I could barely see anything until my eyes adjusted. There were several other strippers working in there. I waved to Jackie. She studied the man, raised one eyebrow, then got back to work.

He sat down on a sofa. Tom left us. I smiled and began to dance in front of him, tugging at the top of my dress.

"No," he said and stopped me.

"Excuse me?"

He shook his head. "Give me a minute. I want to look at you."

What the hell? Look at me? Good grief. I frowned at him and decided he was an asshole. Some guys were. Most just let you do your thing, paid you and went on their way. Others had to get their "money's worth". I figured him for one of those. But I didn't put up with that shit. When I was working, time was money. And he was wasting mine.

"Sorry," I said softly and began to move again. "House rules."

He seemed momentarily stunned by my forwardness. He blinked twice at me, but I didn't stop. I had a job to do and he wasn't going to get in my way.

I moved to the side, rubbing my breasts with one hand. He watched me and settled back into the couch.

"Do you have panties on?" he asked.

I nodded and rubbed my legs.

"Take them off."

I stared at him, almost appalled. Didn't he know that I ran the show? I almost gave up and told him to leave, but then I thought I'd already done about half the show, so why not finish?

I didn't say a word. I widened my stance, bent over, and tugged at the crotch of my panties. Then I looked up at him. He nodded. I pulled them off with one jerk of my hand.

He seemed impressed.

I straddled him then, rubbing my naked crotch up against his and moaned in his ear, then nibbled on it a little. I tugged my dress down and my breasts popped out. He stared down at them, seemingly pleased, and raised one eyebrow when I fingered my nipple, then pinched it. I felt his hand on my ass. I removed it and handed it back to him.

"You can't touch," I said and stopped moving.

He nodded.

I pressed up against him, rubbing my tits in his face and my crotch against his. I suddenly realized, I was wet. I usually didn't get wet because I looked at this as a job. But I was. Wet. I was turned on. And I was getting his expensive suit wet.

That made me want to laugh. Whatever would he tell the dry cleaner? Hell, he'd just get his maid to do it. He wouldn't give a shit what she told him.

He muttered something.

"What?" I asked and looked him in the eye. "I couldn't hear you."

"You're very beautiful."

I smiled. I heard this all the time from my customers. But it seemed different coming from him. I wanted to believe he actually thought it was true and wasn't just using a line on me.

"Thank you."

He nodded and seemed uncomfortable.

I rubbed a little more. Oh, shit. If I kept at this, I wouldn't stop. I'd keep rubbing until I got my groove on, then I wouldn't be able to help myself and I'd come. And I'd never done that before. I'd never wanted to before now. I got an idea. Might include a big tip. Guys loved this kind of thing, right?

I whispered in his ear, "Can I come on your leg?"

His eyebrows shot up.

"Huh?" I said and felt his dick. He was hard. "Can I rub up against your leg and come on it?"

He cleared his throat, then said, "No."

That was *not* the answer I was looking for. What an asshole. Didn't he know how many guys would love for me to do this very thing?

I moved away from him. But I didn't stop rubbing. I liked having control of him. I liked knowing I could do whatever I wanted and he couldn't do a damn thing about it.

"Why not?" I whispered. "Why not let me come on your leg?"

"Because I say so."

Tough shit.

I began to grind against him then, not letting him move. I rubbed my clit in circles against his leg until I could feel the orgasm come at me. I held onto the back of the couch and didn't stop. I rode his leg for all it was worth and it was worth quite a bit. I came then, shivering, and fell against his chest. I stayed there for a moment, wondering why the hell I'd just done that. I mean, I pretended to do it with other guys, but I'd never actually *done* it.

He wasn't pleased. I could just tell. Like I said, most guys would beg me to do that. But not him. He was some type of pervert, I could just tell. There was something wrong with him.

He pushed me off him. I glared up at him and watched as he took out his wallet from his breast pocket, took out some money and threw it on the couch. Then he turned on his heel and left the room without a word.

My face burned. The fucking bastard. I hated him. Which is the exact reason why I began to love him.

Drunk and happy.

He'd come into the club almost nightly after that. He'd sit at the bar with another man, a bigger man, who I presumed to be his bodyguard. He was either his bodyguard or the guy just couldn't relax. He'd keep glancing around the room as if he were casing it. It was almost funny.

They'd watch, but he didn't request any more private shows. Or even a table dance. Fuck him anyway. The way he had acted pissed me off so much that I wanted to tell Tom to kick him and his bodyguard out. I couldn't, of course. Tom wouldn't kick him out unless he *did* something. Of course, he didn't *do* anything. He didn't cause a commotion. He was polite, a good customer. He drank the expensive but watered down drinks and smoked an occasional cigarette. He watched from the sidelines but never participated.

I knew why he came around. I knew he was there for me. And that he'd eventually want to talk to me. Maybe do more. I wasn't interested. I pretended to be uninterested. I was dying to have him talk to me. But he'd have to make the first move.

He didn't for the longest time.

Then one night, I left work early. I had a really bad allergy headache and I couldn't take it anymore. Tom told me to go home. I slipped out the back and thought about getting a taxi, though our apartment was only a few blocks from the club. I decided against it. I didn't like to waste money on stuff like that. Besides, the walk might help my headache.

I got on Bourbon and cut across, walking quickly. The street, as usual, was alive. People were drunk on every corner. Drunk and happy. I ignored them and quickened my pace, wanting an aspirin and bed so bad I could feel it.

I felt a touch on the back of my arm, then at my elbow. Someone was grabbing me, halting me. I automatically jerked my arm because guys always think they can do this kind of stuff in the Quarter. They'll come right up to you and stagger around, grabbing at you like you're a piece of meat. Usually they're drunk off their asses and will mutter stupidly, *"How's about letting me buy you a drink?"*

How's about you fuck off?

"Excuse me?"

I turned around and saw his bodyguard.

"What?" I asked, then held my head. It was throbbing again, aching.

He jerked his head to the side. I looked over at a big, sleek black Mercedes. Limo. His limo. Why do guys like that always have limos? One day, I'd love to see one of them running around in a Pinto. Or a Yugo.

I looked at him. *"And?"*

"He'd like a word. Please?"

"Sorry. I've got to get home," I said and started off.

"Miss?" he called. "Please just do it. For me?"

I stared at him. He seemed almost in a panic. The bastard would probably fire him if he didn't get what he wanted. I nodded and cursed under my breath as I followed him to the car. He held the back door open and I got in.

"Nice to see you," he said before my ass landed on the seat.

"Okay," I said and winced, holding my head. "So what's up?"

"What's wrong?"

"I have a headache," I muttered.

"Would you like an aspirin?"

"No," I said. "What do you want?"

He didn't reply. He was studying me with one raised brow. I gave him his look back, raising a brow myself. He chuckled and looked away.

"What do you want?" I asked again.

"Would you like a ride home?"

I stared at him, breathing in the nice scent of leather from the seats. I couldn't think of a reason *not* to let him give me a ride. Other than the fact that I never let strangers give me rides. But he wasn't really a stranger. Not really.

"Sure," I said and leaned back.

He nodded at the bodyguard, who, apparently, was also his chauffeur. The car rolled forward.

"I live at—"

"I know where you live," he said.

I stared at him, mouth agape. "Really?"

He nodded.

"Is there a reason for that?"

"No," he said.

I rolled my eyes, but didn't pursue it. I didn't care enough about him to pursue it. All I could tell about him was that he was weird. That's the only impression I had. I didn't want to know anything else. I didn't need to.

"By the way," he said, leaning over and extending his hand. "I'm Frank."

Frank. Frank. Franklin. Franklin D. Roosevelt. Frank Sinatra. Frank furters. *Frankly, Mr. Shankly*. FRANK-EN-STEIN.

I eyed his hand. His hands were soft and smooth, his nails clean and trim. He had nice hands. Big. A touch of dark hair on the side. A gold ring on his right pinky, a Rolex watch peeking out from beneath the cuff of his jacket.

Damn. Rich guys like him rarely gave me the time of day. I got the Timex and gold wedding band guys, but not guys like him. Not much anyway. And when I did come across them, they'd turn my stomach. They'd want a dance, maybe want to give me their number or tell me how I could "earn" some extra money, but none of them ever approached me in this kind of manner. None of them let me ride in their fancy cars or offered me aspirin. I guess that was because they all just wanted to use me.

I suddenly felt very uncomfortable.

He hand was still extended. He shook it a little, offering it again. I was almost afraid to take it, but what choice did I have?

I shook his hand and muttered, "Kristy."

"Yeah, I know you name, Kristine."

"Oh," I said off-handedly. "So what do you want?"

He leaned back and seemed to relax. He shot me a quick glance and tried to smile. He failed miserably.

He said, "Nothing. Just thought you'd like a ride home."

He spoke with only a slight Southern accent. I wondered if he'd been brought up in New Orleans. Where did a guy like him come from?

I looked out the window, wishing I'd never gotten in the car. I really wasn't in the mood to play mind games. Hell, I was never in the mood for mind games. Who was? I didn't like being fucked with. And I could tell he was one of those guys who would fuck with you. He'd get a big kick out of driving you crazy, and once you were too far gone, he'd get a big kick out of leaving you flat on your ass.

I decided to mess with him.

"You want to fuck me, don't you?" I asked. "That's what this is all about, isn't it?"

Again, the raised brow, the slight smile combined with a little embarrassment.

"No," he muttered. "I don't suppose that's what I'd call it."

"Then what would you call it?" I asked and leaned over towards him. "Making love?"

He shook his head.

"Screwing?"

He glanced at me. "You've got a mouth on you, don't you?"

"I sure do."

"Were you raised in a trailer park?"

"No," I said. "Were you?"

"Uh, no."

He sighed, as if this was not quite going as he'd planned. He liked control. I could tell that. But so did I.

"Why are you a stripper?" he asked.

"Pays the bills."

He shook his head.

"What?" I asked.

"That's not why you're a stripper."

"It's not?"

He leaned over so our noses were almost touching. I breathed in and smelled him, his cologne, his pheromones. Him. Ahh…Yeah…*No.*

"So why is it?" I breathed.

"You're a stripper because you get to manipulate men."

I pulled back. "I am not."

He nodded. "The first night we met, you wanted to manipulate me."

"I don't do that with everyone," I said and moved away from him.

He grabbed my arm and pulled me back. "No, you don't. You don't do it with everyone because you don't have to. You can get most of these assholes with a bat of your eyes."

"What the hell are you talking about?" I hissed. "And let go of my arm!"

He didn't let go. "You love having men in the palm of your hand, don't you?"

I took a breath and calmed myself down, thinking I could some-how take control of the situation. I placed my hand on his, eased his fingers back gently and freed my arm. He let go of it with only slight reluctance.

"Listen," I said. "I don't know you. You don't know me."

"So?" he asked softly.

"So, you don't have any right to ask me those kinds of questions."

He nodded slightly and took my arm again, pulling me closer. I didn't fight him, I slid over and liked the way our legs touched. I got an electric charge from it, just from that touch.

He muttered, "But you know what I'm talking about. You know exactly what I'm talking about. You get off knowing these men are creaming their pants over you and that they can't touch you, that they'll never have you. You flaunt your sexuality like a badge."

Well, that's one way to put it. I rolled my eyes.

"Am I right?" he asked.

Was he right? Was he? Yeah. He was right. So what?

He released me but didn't shove me away. We sat like that, that close, for a long moment, neither one of us wanting to move. I looked out the window. We were on my street. I was almost disappointed that the ride was almost over.

"You don't like me, do you?" he asked.

I shook my head. "No. I don't really."

He chuckled. "Why?"

Why? *Why didn't I like him?* That was a good question. Maybe it was because he scared me. He scared the hell out of me. It wasn't that I was afraid of him, it was that I was afraid of myself, of what I'd do if he got me under his thumb. I'd never felt like that before. I didn't like the feeling, either.

The car stopped. Just as I reached for the door handle, he leaned over and grabbed me, pulling me back in.

"You feel it, though, don't you?" he whispered.

"Feel what?" I asked and stared into his eyes.

"That energy," he said. "It's undeniable."

"What are you talking about?" I whispercd.

"Sex," he said. "If we had sex, we'd explode."

I looked into his eyes. He was crazier than hell. That's all. He was one crazy motherfucker. But he was right. We would explode. We disliked one another just enough to know that. To know we had it. You don't get it with everyone, that energy, that pure sexual energy. You're lucky if you get it at all.

"You're sick," I told him and meant it.

He nodded. "And you're just like me."

He was probably right.

"Whatever," I replied dryly.

He nodded at me.

I opened the door and got out just as he said, "I'd like you to come to my house for dinner."

I tried to shut the door on him to put an end to this, this impending relationship or fuck fest or whatever it was we were about to embark on. I wanted to run, to try to forget about him and all this sexual energy and his craziness, and push him out of my life by simply closing the door on him. But he held it open.

"I don't think so," I said, knowing that was the best answer, but feeling disappointed by it.

"Tomorrow night," he said.

"I work tomorrow."

"I've already spoken with Tom," he said. "He's giving you the night off."

I leaned down close to him, so close that we were eye to eye, "Let me tell you one thing, I can't be bought. Not by your money, by your looks, your limo, nothing. I'm not that easily impressed. Got it?"

"I'll have Tony pick you up at eight," he said. "And wear something nice."

He eyed my jeans and tanktop. I felt a little uneasy by his look.

"I don't think so," I said and shut the door.

The car immediately pulled away, leaving me to smell its fumes. I noticed that my headache was gone.

The fuck me dress.

Of course I went. How was I, of all people, supposed to turn down an offer like that? I was also as curious as hell. Curious as to what kind of house he lived in and his lifestyle.

And what he'd do once we were alone.

I told myself that I really didn't have a choice. Well, I did have a choice and I knew it, but I pretended I didn't. Besides, I wanted to fuck with him. I wanted that upper hand. I wanted *him* down on his hands and knees, begging for me.

I should have known better.

A beautiful designer dress arrived at my apartment the next day. It was long, black and made entirely of silk. Jackie gasped when I tried it on. I looked like a forties movie star in it. It was that kind of dress.

"That is the most beautiful thing I've ever seen," she said and touched it.

I stared at myself in the mirror. It was beautiful. And it accentuated my curves just right, maybe too right because it made me look like sex, like walking sex, sex on wheels, on heels. It was a fuck me dress. It was perfect. It was so not me. I never wore anything like this, even when I was working. I stuck to the simpler things, like tube-tops and Daisy Dukes. I had the Southern girl thing going, that was my act at the club—the hair in braids, the fresh-faced girl with those oh, so cute freckles. I was the innocent girl who would fuck your brains out on a haystack in the barn. All the men loved it, they ate it up, then they'd come back for more.

Frank must not like the Southern girl thing. Why else would he have sent me this dress? I wouldn't change; he'd have to know that. I was me, that's all I was. Me. I wasn't about to change just because someone sent me a very expensive dress and assumed I'd be over-joyed to wear it. I mean, fuck him. I knew what this was all about.

I tore it off and threw it on the floor. Jackie's eyes almost popped out of her head. She bent over and retrieved the dress from the floor, then held it close to her chest as if she were protecting it.

"Why did you do that?" she snapped.

"It's not my style."

She held the dress up and shook her head. "I think it's beautiful."

That wasn't the point.

"Yeah," I said. "But it's so not me."

She shrugged. "So what?"

"So, it's not me," I said. "I'd never buy anything like that."

"You couldn't afford anything like this."

"Fuck you."

"You know what I mean."

"Well, I'm not wearing it."

"Why not?"

"Because," I said and sighed. "Because he probably thinks he can dress me up and I won't be the person I am at the club."

She stared at me like I was crazy. Maybe I was.

"It's just a dress, Kristy."

"I know! It's just, why would he send that? Like I wouldn't have the sense to know not to come dressed in jeans?"

"You are putting way too much into this."

Was I? Maybe I was. It's just the thought of spending an evening with him—in that dress—was really beginning to bug me. I wouldn't be comfortable in it. No. It wasn't the dress. It was the idea of him, being alone with *him*. I had enough confidence to put that dress on and parade down the street in it. But I didn't have the confidence to parade around in front of him in it. Cause once he saw me in it, I'd know exactly what he'd been thinking. And I'd be thinking the exact same thing. And I didn't want to go there with him. For some reason, I just didn't. He scared me. Sure, there was excitement there too, but there was also something else, something I couldn't put my finger on. Or face up to.

And I knew all I was to him was a conquest. Some guys were like that. They have to have you and once they get you, all you are is a number. Number one, or twelve or twelve-hundred. Doesn't matter which number as long as they can add you to the list. And they fuck you like you're a conquest; it's all about them fucking you. You're just along for the ride. They don't really care if you enjoy it or not, it's all about them, *their* fantasy of you and not you and most certainly not your pleasure.

I didn't want to be a conquest for him. I hated that.

She glanced at me. "I can tell he likes you."

I nodded.

"And he's really cute."

I sighed.

"I think you should go," she said.

"Why?"

"I dunno," she said with a sigh, then sat down next to me.

I smiled at her. She was little, so tiny, with a cute pixie haircut that drove men wild. Though she was my age, she looked sixteen. Or younger. All the old men in the club loved her.

"It's just..." she began. "It's just an adventure. It's not everyday you get asked out by a guy like that."

"What kind of guy do you think he is?"

She shrugged. "I dunno."

"Do you think he might be a pervert?"

She burst out laughing. "No! What makes you think that?"

I thought about the first night I met him, me coming on his leg, him getting pissed off. I didn't say anything. Maybe I was the pervert.

"Nothing," I said and stared out the window.

"Look, he seems nice. He's probably just reserved or shy or something. Go have some fun and see what happens."

I nodded.

"And wear the dress."

"Why?"

"Because no man could resist you in that dress."

She had a point.

"But—" I began.

"Stop it," she said and threw the dress in my lap. "Wear it tonight and give him some major blue balls."

I grinned at her. "Okay."

"And the next time you see him, he'll be begging at your feet."

I stared at her. What a wonderful idea.

Absolutely beautiful.

Five minutes before eight, his limo pulled up. Jackie gave me a wink and a smile just before I threw open the door and ran down the stairs. Actually, I didn't run. You don't run in five inch heels. You walk. Slowly.

Tony, the chauffeur/bodyguard, had just opened the foyer door when I got to it. We stared at each other until I burst out laughing.

"I was just coming for you," he muttered.

I nodded. "I know. I guess I just got ahead of myself."

He nodded and held the door open so I could pass in front of him. Then he raced to the car and opened the back door in a hurry. I smiled at him and got in. He shut the door and we were on our way.

Frank's house was located in the Garden District. Yeah, I had a feeling he lived there. He lived in a three story, Georgian-style mansion that was called the Chandler House. It was that old, old enough to have it's own name and big enough to dwarf the other mansions that sat beside it.

It was magnificent. I hate to admit it, but I was in awe. Stupefied. I never expected to be invited to one of these houses. And my poor, pitiful apartment that I had painstakingly cleaned and decorated with used furniture and flea market finds just looked like a rathole next to it. Before I saw his house, I'd actually thought I had a nice place.

I pretended to be unimpressed. I closed my slack jaw and told myself it wasn't *that* big. I'd seen bigger. And better.

The driver opened the door and I proceeded up the walk, up the steps, and to the door. I had just held out my finger to ring the bell when the butler suddenly opened the door. I jerked back.

"Good evening, mademoiselle," he said with a French accent. "Monsieur awaits you."

So formal. I tried not to roll my eyes because he seemed like a nice old guy. I gave him a friendly smile and followed him into the study. I also tried not to gasp at the size of the "front hall" or at all the expensive artwork or antiques or at the size of the double grand staircase.

It was just all so *gigantic.*

I affected an air of detachment and followed the butler. Frank was in a massive wing chair in front of a huge stone fireplace. He jumped up when we came in. The butler bowed and exited the room backwards, shutting the door softly on his way out.

I could tell he was at once pleased at my appearance. And with the dress. I knew I looked good. He knew it too. I was glad to see *he* had noticed. If he hadn't, well, let's just say, *I* wouldn't have been pleased.

"Good to see you," he said, eyeing me, my ass in particular.

I gave him a grin. "Good to see you, too."

"I see you got the dress."

I turned around, then back. "Yeah. Thanks."

He nodded. "Oh, no problem. You look absolutely beautiful."

Absolutely beautiful. I almost blushed. Yeah. He'd just said that. Absolutely beautiful. Best damn compliment I'd ever received.

"Thank you," I said and smiled a little.

"Would you like a drink?"

"Sure," I said and sat down in the chair opposite his. "Whatever you're having."

He smiled slightly, then went over to the bar, where he poured me a glass of champagne. Dom Perignon. I took it, sipped and smiled. Damn, that was good stuff.

He sat down in the other chair, leaning forward. I finished my champagne.

"Would you like another?" he asked.

I shook my head, feeling somewhat uncomfortable.

"Sure?"

"Yes, I'm sure."

God, I was so intimidated, I was rendered shy. I'd never been shy in all of my life.

We didn't try to make conversation. We couldn't have conversed if our lives depended on it. My heart was beating so fast. I wondered if his was doing the same? He gave me an uncomfortable smile, then leaned over and lit my cigarette when I pulled one out of my tiny evening purse.

"Thanks," I muttered.

He smiled. I attempted to smile back. I was nervous. The room shook with silence. The only noise I could hear was the occasional jingle of the trolley outside. And that was far off.

The butler knocked on the door, opened it and announced, "Dinner is served."

Frank stood, walked over to me and held out his elbow. I almost cracked up. I didn't. I put my cigarette out, grabbed my purse and took his arm. I liked the way it felt, too, his arm. Strong. It felt strong. Stern. He had strong, stern arms.

We followed the old man into the massive dining room/hall/big motherfucking room. The table was about twenty feet long, lined with elegant chairs, some of which looked like they needed recovering.

I sat down to his right, instead of at the end of the long table, which I would have preferred. We didn't speak as we were served some kind of soup, which I did not like, then some kind of duck, which I picked at, then some fluffy, chocolate thing, which I devoured.

Once the plates were removed, he leaned back and pulled a cigar out of his jacket. He offered it to me. I shook my head and pulled my cigarettes out. He leaned over and lit my cigarette, then his cigar, which he twirled in his fingers until it was totally red on the end and smoked like a chimney.

We smoked and still didn't say a damn thing. I couldn't take it anymore. I looked around the room, racking my brain trying to come up with something to say, then I stared at the chairs.

"Why don't you recover these chairs?" I asked. "They'd look really good recovered."

He had been sucking on the cigar when I said this. His eyebrows shot up. I could tell he got a kick out of my question and he tried to hide his laughter, like I amused him. Like what I had said was such a sweet, silly little thing.

"What's so funny?" I asked, somewhat stupefied.

He shook his head and explained, not really in a condescending way, "When you purchase antiques, you don't reupholster them. You leave them the way they are."

I glared at him. How in the hell was I supposed to know that?

"I was wondering if you would ask me that," he said in a manner that made me think he wanted to lean over and pinch my cheeks.

I blushed. I felt insulted, though I don't think he meant it as an insult. Suddenly, I wanted out of there so bad I could have jumped up and ran to the door. I couldn't take the tension anymore. It was eating me alive.

He took the cigar out of his mouth, then wiped the tip of his tongue with his fingers and flicked a piece of tobacco from them, like some actor. I rolled my eyes at his behavior. Why was he putting on a show? Was he putting on a show? And what did he want? Was it just sex? Or a game, something to divert his attention from his lush, but apparently boring life. What was his deal?

And what was mine? I was impressed. I've got no problem admitting that. But I knew he'd never give me anything. Nothing. I'd go with what I came, maybe without so much of my pride. Maybe I'd lose part of my heart, too. But I couldn't imagine loving this guy. No matter how good looking or rich he was. No matter. It didn't matter to me. I could take it or leave it.

So why was I still sitting here?

"It's getting late," I said, sighed and began to stand. "I should really be going."

He touched my arm, making me stop. I shivered at his touch. My heart picked up its pace, from steady to skipping, then thumping, pounding, until it swam in my head. I couldn't think straight. For a moment, all I could think about was his hand on my arm. And how it felt being there.

I moved away from him. Quickly.

"Why don't we sit in front of the fire? In the study? I had Pierre make a fire." "That's very romantic," I said. "But I'm not in the mood."

His eyes narrowed at me. I'd pissed him off. I didn't really care, though. I was tired. This had really turned out to be nothing more than a dud with him being the main dud of the evening. I didn't like the fancy food or the fancy cigar or the fancy house. I liked comfort, hamburgers, soft chairs. I'd never, ever be able to get comfortable here, in this house. And I knew it.

Like I said, I was intimidated. I was out of my element. Maybe that was his whole reason in bringing me here. I didn't have the energy to speculate, though. I just didn't care. I told myself I didn't care.

"Please," he said. "Just for a moment or two?"

I really didn't want to. But his look implored me. It made me change my mind. After all, he had been nice tonight. Not really overly friendly or anything, but he had been nice. Which was more than I had expected.

"I guess," I muttered.

He rose from his chair, extended his arm. I didn't want to take it. I didn't want to touch him again. But it wouldn't be polite if I refused. I took it and we went into the study, where there was now a huge fire crackling and steaming in the fireplace. It did give the room a sort of rosy glow. The fire made the room a little less imposing. Not much, but some.

We sat side by side on the big leather sofa and stared vacantly at the fire. At least I did. I knew he was studying me, like he studied me at the club and in his car.

I turned to him. "What are you doing?"

"Nothing," he said and rested his hand on the side of his face. "I'm just looking at you."

"No, that's not what I meant," I said. "Why did you invite me here?"

"I like your company."

"Bull," I said. "You haven't said two words to me all evening."

"I think I've said at least two," he said, his eyes twinkling. "Maybe even three."

I tried not to be charmed. "I know what it's about, Frank."

"What?"

"This. I know why you wanted me to come here."

"You do?" he asked, and seemed more than a little curious.

I nodded. "It's about sex, isn't it?"

His eyebrows rose. "Uh, no, I don't—"

I scooted closer to him. "Listen, I know you want me. It's okay, a lot of guys do. But I don't need pretension."

"I'm not pretentious. This is just the way I am."

He was right. It didn't make me feel any more comfortable, but I still wanted to know something, and I was going to say it, even if it embarrassed me to death, I was going to ask.

"Why do you want to fuck me so bad?"

He eyes darted up, then down. "Who says I do?"

"Oh come on," I said, moving even closer to him, so close I could feel the warmth from his body. "You've had a hard-on for me since the minute you laid eyes on me."

"I don't have a hard-on right now."

"Really?" I said and eyed his crotch. He was right. There was no tent in his pants. "Just tell me why."

"You're very independent, aren't you, Kristine?"

"What?"

He moved closer to me. "You like being a stripper because you think it makes you superior to men. Am I right?"

I thought about it. I did take his assumption into consideration. But he was full of shit. I liked being a stripper because I liked the money.

"No, you're not right," I said and moved away from him. "Besides, we've already had this discussion once before."

"I know that."

"So give it up."

"Like I said before, you love having guys want you."

He took my arm and wouldn't let it go. I tried to jerk away, but he held tight.

"You like having all the power don't you, Kristine?"

"Don't call me that," I said. "No one calls me that."

"They should," he said. "It's a lovely name."

"Let me go."

I elbowed him. I suddenly wanted out of there more than before. If I didn't get out, there would be no going back. I knew that. I struggled against him, pushing him away, but he wouldn't let me go.

He pulled me back down and we began to wrestle for a moment until I grabbed his crotch.

"Like that?" I hissed. "You're right. I love having guys by the balls."

I gave him a slight squeeze, just enough to get his attention so he'd know I could do more. He didn't flinch, only reached over and grabbed me by the hair of the head and pulled me back. I winced in pain. It hurt so much tears sprang into my eyes.

"OW!" I yelled. "Let me go!"

"That's what you like, isn't it?" he whispered hotly in my ear. I could feel his saliva.

I pushed him away and wiped my ear.

He pulled me back. "The only man that you're interested in is one that treats you like shit, isn't it? The one who can dominate you?"

I didn't know. I'd never really had a man try to dominate me before. They, all five of my ex-boyfriends and the one ex-husband included, had been like putty in my hands. I could manipulate them in any way I chose. And they had bored me to tears. That's why I was single. Why I hadn't just settled down with one of them and lived my life like a normal person. They had been too easy. Too easy to get, to have, to contain. I'd tempt them sometimes, yell at them, scream, do anything just so they would flare up. Just to test them. Every once in while, I'd get what I wanted. Once I got a black eye. But he had cried like a baby after he gave it to me and told me he would have rather have cut off his hands than hurt me, even offered to do it. I had run away from him, using the black eye as an excuse for escape.

From what I heard, he still has his hands.

Frank stared me dead in the eye. I stared back and waited for him to do something. We stayed like that for what seemed like a long time. Our chests pressed close, our hearts beating wildly in our chests. We waited until one of us made a move. We waited for each other to make the first move. I decided to go ahead and do it, since I didn't want to be there all night.

This time, I twisted his balls. He let out a wail and released me.

"You bitch," he hissed and pushed me away from him hard.

I fell to the floor. I stared up at him just as my emotions began to run wild. I went from embarrassment to shock to anger to loathing.

"Fuck you," I said, getting up from the floor. I felt a lump rise in my throat. I was almost in tears. I was also very angry, mostly because I realized that he did have me all figured out. To a certain extent.

He eyed me dispassionately. I hated that look on his face. I hated that I didn't have him figured out as he had me.

"Fuck you," I spat and felt the tears puddle in my eyes and fall on my face. "Fuck you! Fuck you! *FUCK YOU!*"

His look changed. He almost grinned at me. He loved my anger, my seething passion. He knew I was just a touch or two away from ignition.

"Yeah, come on, then, fuck me," he said and eyed me. "Come on."

"Right!" I scoffed. "Don't you ever touch me again, mother-fucker!"

He looked up at me. "Your pussy tells on you, Kristine. It's all wet, wanting this motherfucker in there fucking you."

He reached out for me. Before I knew what he was doing, his hand was up my dress. I didn't have any panties on. You don't wear panties with a dress like this. I wish I had. I wish I had because his hand was between my legs and there was nothing there to stop him. He was fingering me there and he was right. I told on myself. I was wet for him. For him. In this moment. Here. I was wet and I wanted him more than anything.

He knew it. I knew it. It didn't stop me from hating myself for an instant, then reverting back to hating him.

He didn't say a word as he stroked me. As he fingered my clit, the lips of my pussy, which swelled and yearned for him to do more. But he didn't. He sat a foot away from me with his hand up my dress and finger fucked me. Finger fucked me until I was dissolving into a mass of quivering nerves. Until I moaned and pushed myself against his hand. His hand rested. It became still. I moved against it, feeling my own hands on my breasts, wanting his lips there more than anything. Wanting him. I fucked his hand which waited patiently for me to do as I wanted. And just as I was about to come, he pulled it away.

I gasped and opened my eyes. "You bastard."

He grinned at me. A real shit eating grin. I hated him.

"So tell me I was right."

Before I could change my mind, I slapped him. I slapped him right across the face. He didn't move. He did raise one eyebrow. But that's all he did.

I shoved him away and headed to the door. I was so mad I could have spit. I did spit. Right on his Persian rug. I was almost ashamed after I did it, but I couldn't help myself.

He was suddenly on me, on my back, shoving me to the floor. He was on top of me, pulling at my dress, trying to get it off. I rolled over and kicked him right in the head. He fell back with a thump and a groan. I scrambled up and hobbled in my five inch heels to the front door. I'd never wear these things out again. But before I could turn the knob, he was at me, pulling me down, holding me tight and not letting me move.

"OFF!" I screamed as he turned me around.

"Tell me," he whispered.

"Tell you what!"

"Tell me how much you want me."

"Get off me!" I screamed and pushed at him.

"Come on, baby," he whispered, his hot breath on my ear. "Tell me how much you want me."

I stared at him.

"Come on. Tell me."

Tell me, tell me now. Tell me how low I can go. Beat me there. Hold me down. Fight with me. Kiss me. Kiss me now. Bite me. Scratch me. Make me want you. Take me away. Don't ever leave. Do what you want to me. With me. Fuck me. Fuck me now. *Make me feel alive.*

He was waiting. I tried to turn away from him. I tried to turn it all off, all the emotions I had were running riot inside me then. I wanted him. I knew it. He knew it. There was no going back.

I was still breathing hard. He was still waiting.

I breathed, "I want you."

"How much?"

"I don't know," I breathed. "I just want you so bad."

"You want me to fuck you?"

I nodded.

"Beg me."

I almost regained my senses. But I realized this was his game. This is what he wanted, what he got off on. I also realized, I liked it, too. And I was willing to play along.

"Please fuck me."

"Really beg me."

"Please fuck me!"

"More."

"Please, please, please! Please, fuck me. Fuck me—"

I didn't have time to finish. He covered my lips with his. He was sucking the life right out of me, thrusting his hateful tongue deep into my mouth and down my throat. I pushed at him and struggled. I could barely breathe. But he kept kissing. He kept kissing, sucking, groaning, moaning. He was right. I was wet. I did want his cock in me. I didn't melt. I exploded. I panted with lust for him, grabbing his face and holding him tight so he couldn't get away.

I suddenly wondered where the butler was. I didn't wonder long. I was too into it to wonder about anything but having him on me, in me, fucking my brains out.

He was coming out of his clothes. I was coming out of mine. I don't even know how we got them off. But there they were, strewn all over the floor and he was kissing all of my naked body, which arched under his rough and desperate touch. He pawed at me like an animal, biting at my skin until I was covered with tiny red marks. His head went between my legs and he sucked my cunt, sucked the juices right out of it and into his mouth. I gasped and rode his head, fucked his head until I screamed with orgasm. Until I screamed with liberation.

Then he was in me, fucking me. His cock went right up in me like it had always been there and he was simply returning it. I gasped with satisfaction. I gasped for him. For the moment. For the fucking. And he was fucking me then. Fucking me like no other man had ever fucked me. He was fucking another orgasm right out of my body. I held on tight and rode him as he rode me, taking it for everything it was worth and refusing to let it go until I was so spent I couldn't move.

He came then, shuddered, fell on top of me and didn't move for a long moment. He held onto me tight, like he was never going to move, never going to let me go. I found my arms holding him too, holding him like I loved him and never wanted to let him go. And I knew, I knew I wasn't just a conquest fuck for him. There was something else there. I didn't know what it was, but that hadn't been a conquest fuck. It had been about us, me and him, fucking. He wasn't looking to add me to his list. And that made me just a tad apprehensive. What did he want with me?

He said, "I want you to move in."

The scary part.

I'll use him. That was my first thought.

The choice was easy after that. I made my decision that night and moved in the next day. Jackie raised one eyebrow.

"Why are you moving in with this guy?" she asked. "You just, like, met him a few weeks ago."

I told her truthfully, "I'm going to use him."

She studied me. "Do you love him?"

Did I? No! Of course I didn't love him. I didn't even really know him that well. But what did that matter? I knew about him. I knew I liked fucking him. That was good enough. For now.

"No! I'm just going to use him. He knows that."

"You just met him, Kristy."

You said that once already.

"Kristy?"

"I know," I said, shifting my feet.

I mean, I knew it was all of a sudden and Frank was almost a stranger. I knew it wasn't really rational of me to just move in with him, but something told me to. Something was pushing me towards him and I was helpless to do anything other than hold on for the ride.

She narrowed her eyes at me. "Well, if that's what you want."

I nodded. It was.

She sighed. "Well, shit. Who the hell can I get to move in?"

I stared at her.

"I can't pay this rent by myself, you know?"

"I'll help you until you find someone."

She eyed me. "Yeah. Right. But can you find someone to take your place?"

I didn't know. I really didn't care. I was ready to sprint to Frank.

"I'll help you," I said and smiled at her. "I promise."

She eyed me. "Let me tell you one thing, though, okay?"

I nodded.

"If he ever hurts you, I know people."

"What do you mean?"

"I mean, I know people who can put him back in his place."

I nodded, getting her meaning.

"He's not like that," I said.

"You never know," she said.

That was true. You never know.

I moved in because I felt it was the right thing to do. I told myself I'd use him, his mansion and his money. And that's exactly what I did. He gave me everything I wanted. I'd call my girlfriends up and we'd go shopping. He never set a limit on my spending, but he did set a limit on my friendships. Quickly, I was told when to be home and that I was to quit my job at the club.

I laughed in his face. "I have to earn a living."

"You're living here."

"But for how long? How long before you get tired of our fucking and kick me out?"

"I won't get tired of it."

I eyed him. "Then set me up a bank account. I want money."

He eyed me. "You sound like a whore."

Maybe it did sound that way, but, shit, I had the stripper mentality. Men were there to be used and most times, they liked being used.

As long as they were getting something out of it, everyone was happy. And he was getting a little more than something. He was getting me. And I wasn't cheap.

"I don't care what I sound like. I won't quit my job without a little security. Why should I?"

"You've got a point," he said.

He set it up the next day, depositing a lot of fucking money into an account, which I immediately transferred into another account, so he couldn't take it back if he changed his mind. But he didn't care about the money. He only wanted me under his control, under his thumb. Besides, I knew if he wanted that money back, he'd get it. And I really didn't care about it. I just told him to do it to see if he would. When he did, I almost fell over in shock.

What else could I get him to do if I asked?

The sex got better. Unbelievably, it got better. I didn't know if I was in love with him or in love with his dick. Maybe it was his hands that I loved. They were large, like his dick. They pawed at me, forced me to be still, quiet, then to move again. I'd never had a man fuck me like he fucked me. I worried that he might cut me off. That he might tire of me too soon. And then what would I do? What would I do with this addiction to his body?

I didn't know. And that was the scary part.

Run of the house.

I soon began to notice that my friends were slipping away. Bit by bit, I was losing contact with them. I invited them over to the house. They came, admired it, then left. I got the feeling that they thought I was feeling my importance and acting snobbish. That was just stupid. I knew this shit wasn't going to last. I was only making the best of it. But most of my friends were strippers and most of them had little education, which made them feel intimidated, which made them act like bitches. Which, in turn, left me feeling a little indignant. It also made me not want anything to do with them.

Jackie did keep in contact. I called her everyday. We'd make pleasant conversation and we'd sometimes go shopping or to lunch, but she couldn't be with me everyday. She did have a life of her own and couldn't entertain me all the time.

I became lonely, living mostly by myself because Frank was always gone somewhere on business. And when he was home, he was never in the mood to talk. But neither was I.

I took control of the house. I had the run of it, so I figured, I'd make it more comfortable for me. I had the cook make all the fattening good food I loved: Hot dogs, burgers, pizzas. Beer. I'd eat whatever I wanted for lunch, then I'd eat with him at dinner, picking at my food because it was always some strange concoction that looked and smelled as unappealing as it tasted.

I picked a room on the main floor and turned it into my own personal pad. It was smaller than the other rooms, but that didn't make it puny, by anyone's standards. It had two camel-backed sofas sitting opposite one another before a huge stone fireplace. It had a bear rug on the polished wood floor, floor to ceiling bookshelves, and a huge executive desk in the corner. I loved it because it was painted a dark red and had thick, lush blue velvet curtains on the windows.

I not only picked that room because I liked the way it looked, I picked it because Frank never went into it.

I had a big screen TV and a DVD player delivered. He didn't have cable (who knows why?) so I had that installed. I also got a laptop and would surf the internet for hours to kill time between fuckings.

I got to know the cook pretty well. She was a native of New Orleans and liked working for Frank, though at first she had a hard time with the menus he wanted. She was a very nice lady, who talked a mile a minute and cracked up all the time. She told funny stories about her six grandkids. She was about fifty-eight. Her name was Ellen and she arrived at the house at five in the morning to cook his breakfast, stayed during the day to cook my lunch, and left just after she finished supper.

She was off on weekends.

Pierre, the butler, kept his distance. But he was always lurking around to see what I was up to, like he was waiting for me to do something so he could tell Frank on me. He got on my nerves so bad. He didn't do shit, either. He was just there to announce dinner, say hello and goodbye and to open the fucking door. I never got used to it. Every single time I came home, I'd reach for the door but he'd already have it open, thusly scaring the shit out of me. *Every single time.*

The chauffeur, Tony, was always with Frank. I'd only see him if we went out to dinner. He was very polite, but kept his distance. He was a young guy, around my age and every so often, I'd see him staring at my legs or ass. Occasionally, when I had a short skirt on, I'd hike it up a little so he could get a peek of ass. Needless to say, he was a little friendlier on the days I wore a short skirt.

The only other person in the house was the maid. She came once a day, made the beds, cleaned the bathrooms and did a little dusting here and there. She didn't have time to talk and when I asked her what her name was, she snapped, "Gloria! Now get out of my way! I'm trying to vacuum!"

I got out of her way.

A team of maids came once a week to do the harder cleaning and they didn't want anything to do with me, either.

So, mostly, I was all by myself. I filled my time reading trashy novels,

surfing the internet, taking baths, shopping, and fantasizing about sex with Frank.

I don't know what Frank did during the day. I don't know how he got that house or all that money. He never divulged any information and I never pressed. I pretended that he was involved with the Mob, or ran a meth lab in the projects. I'd come up with all kinds of underhanded stuff he could be doing to be so rich. I also suspected that he inherited a great deal of what he had. Which was realistic, but boring. When Jackie asked one day, I said, "Well, I think he's distributes cocaine. He's always flying to Colombia, so you never know…"

Actually, I never knew where he was or where he went or how he got there. After a while, I stopped asking. I mean, what was the use? He wasn't going to tell me, so I gave up.

I'd also visit my old haunts, run into friends, then run back and wait for his return.

Like I said, I was bored out of my skull.

This went on for a little while. It was fun, at first, to have no responsibilities, to be kept. To sleep till whenever I wanted, then do whatever I wanted. The fun didn't last. Soon, I was bored out of my skull. I'd run out of the house, jump into my '75 Camaro, and hit the road, sometimes bypassing the city limits and always being tempted to stay on that road all the way home. One day, I got as far as Alabama. But I turned around.

P-A-R-T-Y.

Jackie said, "You know what you should do?"

"No. What?"

"You should throw a huge party."

I shrugged and picked a piece of pepperoni off my pizza. "I dunno. I don't think Frank would like that."

"Well, he's going to be gone all week, isn't he?"

I nodded sadly. Yeah, all week. I'd begged him not to go, to stay or to at least take me with him. "But you'd just be bored," he said. "And I wouldn't get any work done."

That was true.

"So why not have a kickass party?" she asked. "We could put streamers up and invite everyone we know and get some good tunes, some good food and have a really good time."

Sounded like a good idea to me.

"I mean, what's the use in having this great house at your disposal if you're not going to throw a party every once in a while?"

"That's true."

"See? I told you it was a good idea."

"Yeah, it is," I said, really liking the idea of a party now. "Who could we invite?"

"Well, everyone at the club, for sure, except for Jeanie, cause she is such a bitch."

"You got that right."

"And, of course Chad."

Chad, my former neighbor. He was such a nice guy and had a crush on me, though he never asked me out. I always wondered why he hadn't.

"How is Chad?"

"He's heartbroken since you moved out."

I grinned. "Really?"

"Really," she said but didn't venture. "And, let's see, some other people I know from around the neighborhood. I don't see inviting more than say…thirty people."

"That's not so bad."

"No," she said. "And we'll have it all cleaned up before he comes home and he'll never know."

"You're right," I said. "That would be fun! I need to mingle with someone other than Pierre."

"He's the butler, right?"

I nodded. "Yeah."

She rolled her eyes. I rolled mine.

"So are we on?" she asked.

"Yeah! Let's do it!"

"Cool!" she said.

"When?"

"How about Friday night?"

"Friday night it is!"

She considered something, then said, "Shit. I'm supposed to work Friday night."

I stared at her.

"Oh, fuck it. I'll call in sick."

"That's my girl."

❦   ❦   ❦

I hired a caterer, got a few kegs, which looked ridiculous in the elegant house, and put a bunch of hard rock CDs in the stereo. Jackie and I moved a long sofa table in the foyer and lined it with liquor, glasses and ice. Then we hung streamers from the ceiling, set out a bunch of extra ashtrays, and filled the dining room table with all the good food the caterer supplied.

We got party favors, which included: silly little hats, fake Rolex watches, dancing hula girls and bags of oregano which were supposed to look like pot. For a joke. (They were all gone first thing, then I found them discarded all over the house.)

It was the most fun I'd had since I'd moved in. The guests began to arrive around seven that Friday night.

Pierre and Tony stood around, shaking their heads, telling me that Frank would not be happy about this. *At all.* I shrugged happily and said, "It's not my idea, sorry." Besides, I wanted to have fun and I wanted everyone that came to have fun. I wanted them to eat too much, drink too much and then vomit off the porch.

In a matter of hours, the house was full of people. More than thirty. Way more than thirty. Apparently, everyone who had been invited had invited everyone they knew. But, I figured, that made it more fun. I was so happy to see everyone, even people I'd never met. I'd been sequestered for too long. I needed this. I got drunk on rum punch and mingled happily with everyone, who seemed to be having just a good time as I was. We were loud and obnoxious. We had AC/DC playing on the stereo. Someone cranked up *Back in Black* so loud that one of the speakers blew out and actually smoked.

When I saw it happen, I thought it was the funniest damn thing. I doubled over with laughter. I had been standing by the speaker, screaming along with the song when it happened. I was momentarily shocked. Then I just cracked up. Just looking at the demolished speaker made me laugh. I laughed and laughed and all these people stared at me, then they joined in and we laughed together, rolling on the floor.

Rum punch will do that kind of thing to you. It's good shit.

I can't remember much after that. But I do remember that Frank came home around two that morning. He had canceled part of his trip so he could be home. With me. And not with a few hundred of my nearest and dearest, most of whom I had never met.

The party was still roaring. I was so drunk, I was on the verge of throwing up over the stairs. I had been trying to mount the stairs and get to bed for the last half-hour, but I kept getting stopped by people who told me, *This is the best party they'd been to in years!* ("Glad you like it!") And, *Did I want a little coke?* ("Uh, no thanks.") And, *Where is the bathroom?* ("Up the stairs, to the left.")

I finally gave up and sat down on a step, ready to hurl. My head was spinning a little, too. No, it was spinning anymore. It had taken off and was now lost in space, orbiting Earth.

I don't know where Jackie went. She was probably off in one of the bedrooms getting fucked. Good for her. I was just about to force myself up off the step, retire to my bedroom and leave the party to wind down on its own. I mean, there as no way I was going to break up a party that good. No way. That would be, like, sacrilege.

Then Frank came in. The look on his face was murderous.

I was about halfway up the stairs and had just glanced down at the door when I saw him. My heart leaped a little. I was actually happy to see him and was about to rush down the stairs and throw my arms around him when I realized that Pierre and Tony had been right. He was not happy about the party. Or about what the guests were doing.

Then he did an odd thing. He turned on his heel and left the house. I was bewildered by his behavior, then I suddenly retched, throwing up on the stairs, all over the carpet that covered then. Oh, no. He wouldn't be happy about that either.

What should I do? Run? Yeah, I should. But right now, I should sit down on the steps and hold my buzzing head in my hands. Maybe then I could walk and, then, possibly, run.

I don't know how long I sat there, but suddenly, the entire house was in chaos. A team of cops burst into the front door and announced that the party was *OV-ER!* and that everyone there was trespassing and to *GET THE FUCK OUT!*

I briefly wondered if I should follow suit. But after I got over my initial shock, I got pissed off.

That bastard! He had called the cops! Like we were squatters or something. My drunken mind didn't rationalize. I just thought, *He can't do this! He has no right, even if it was his house!*

I looked for him but he was nowhere in sight. And everyone was emptying the house at an alarmingly quick pace. Where was Jackie? Oh, there she was, trying to pull her shirt over her head as she flew out the front door. She stopped, spotted me and gave a little wave. I lamely waved back.

I watched in dismay as everyone else followed suit. Out they went, pushing at each other, as if they couldn't leave quick enough, as if the house were on fire or something. Out through the front door, out the back. I saw a few hop out of the windows. I saw people grab bottles of champagne, of liquor, and a few even took some really expensive knickknacks, which made me smile.

I put my head back in my hands and closed my eyes. Next thing I knew, someone was tugging at my elbow. I opened my eyes to see Tony, who smiled gently at me, almost with a sense of pity.

"Come on," he said gently. "You need to get to bed."

I allowed him to pull me up the stairs, then into the bedroom, where he pushed me on the bed gently, took off my high heels, then propped a pillow under my head.

"Thank you, Tony," I muttered and closed my eyes.

He muttered something.

"What?"

"Nothing," he said. "Just try to get some rest."
I fell asleep almost immediately.

Bad girl.

Upon Frank's return, I was given a beating.

I really didn't even suspect he would ever do anything like that. I mean, we had good sex and sometimes he'd pull my hair and bite at my neck, and, of course, he spanked me, especially after I'd been a "bad girl", but I'd been the one to initiate that. However, I never in a million years thought he'd beat me.

But he did.

I was asleep. The house was now calm. I knew there was a big mess waiting for me to clean up, but I'd get to it the next day. Right then, the only thing on my mind was sleep. Which was the only thing that would relieve the bed spins I was now in the midst of.

Frank stomped into the bedroom about five that morning. He threw on all the lights and was cursing up a storm.

"Who in the motherfucking hell do you think you are, you stupid, worthless little cunt! Do you have any idea what you've done!"

I opened one eye and was still too drunk to be disturbed by his behavior. Like I've said, he was weird to being with so nothing he did ever really worried me. That was just the way he was.

"You've been given too much control in our relationship," he said and stopped beside the bed, hands on hips. "I have to take it back."

I stared at him, then moaned, "Can we talk in the morning? I don't feel so good."

He snatched the bed covers off me. "Get up!"

I groaned but didn't move. Actually, I *couldn't* move.

"GET UP!" he roared.

I grabbed the blanket and tried to cover myself. He pulled it off the bed and threw it on the floor.

"Get up now, Kristine," he said, more calmly. "You're only making this worse."

"What the hell are you talking about?" I murmured, wishing he'd go away. No, wishing he'd get in bed with me and hold me. I'd carried an ache around with me since the day he'd left—the previous Tuesday. I'd missed him so much that all I wanted was for him to kiss my cheek, hold me tight and mutter, "Good night." We could have sex later, when I felt better. But all I wanted now was his arms around me.

Besides, I was still partially asleep. And I kinda thought he was playing a game with me. I didn't really think he was *that* mad. Sure, I could see why he would be pissed off, but I didn't think he was seeing red or anything. I also didn't think the house was that trashed. (Later, I would fully realize the extent of the damage to the house and feel really bad about it.)

When he didn't respond, I began to fall back asleep, smiling slightly at how good it felt and noticing how warm and cozy the bed was.

He wasn't having that.

He leaned over and shook me awake. Shook me so hard, my head rolled. I screamed and swatted at him, like a bear not wanting to come out of hibernation and getting good and pissed off that someone would try to make me.

"Are you awake?" he hissed in my face, spitting on me.

"You bastard!" I yelled and wiped my face with the back of my hand. "I'm up! What do you want!"

"Take off your clothes," he said.

I eyed him. He had to be joking.

"Do you want sex?" I asked, feeling disgusted with him if he did. I know I looked like hell. And I smelled like a wino.

He shot me a look of pure disdain.

"What then?" I asked.

He turned away form me and pulled off his belt. "Take your clothes off."

"Excuse me?"

"Take your clothes off."

He had to be out of his mind. What was he doing? Undressing? No, he just had his belt off and was slapping it slightly against his thigh. I stared at the belt, then at him, trying to figure this thing out. What *was* his intention? Was he…? No. He didn't intend on beating me, did he?

He did.

He stared back at me, unblinking. I looked away and felt a sudden rush of pure dread come over my body. *What have I done? What was I doing here? Could I get out of it? What was he going to do with that belt?*

"What's the belt for?" I asked, eying it, especially the thick, silver buckle.

"You know."

"Tell me."

He didn't respond. I decided to try something.

I pouted and made my bottom lip quiver like I was about to cry. This usually really got to him. He stared at me and rolled his eyes.

"That's not going to work tonight."

"Come on, baby," I pouted. "I know I've been bad, but I can make it up to you."

"Like I said, that is not going to work."

"Frank—"

"Kristine, take your fucking clothes off!"

I slid off the bed and walked over to him. "Why? What are you going to do if I do?"

"You're going to find out."

His voice was so icy it sent shivers up my spine.

"Now, be a *good* girl and take your clothes off."

It finally dawned on me. He was serious. He was actually going to beat me.

"You are not doing this," I muttered. "Why are you doing this?"

"Kristine, take your clothes off."

"Frank, you don't want to do this to me."

"I have to. You know that."

"But *why*?" I asked, almost crying, and this time I wasn't faking it. "Are you going to hit me?"

He nodded. "Yes. I am going to hit you."

"But why do you want to hit me?" I cried, shaking my head, trying to figure out if this was really happening or if he was playing some sort of sick joke.

"Because you deserve it."

If I hadn't been terrified, I would have laughed. Right in his face. But I was petrified. I was scared shitless. I glanced at the door. I glanced at him, formulated my escape route and his response to the escape route.

I'd give him one last chance to redeem himself. I walked over to the bed and laid down and stared at him seductively.

"If you want them off, you'll have to do it yourself."

"You're making this worse."

"Are you out of your mind?" I asked.

"No, Kristine, I'm not," he said and sighed. "Now you either get up off that bed and undress or I will drag you off it."

That did it. I shot up and ran to the door. I ran with all my might, with everything I could, that fight or flight instinct carrying me and carrying me with haste.

I reached the door, grabbed the knob and turned. It was locked.

I whirled around and stared at him in terror. He stared back, his face devoid of emotion. I swallowed hard and wanted to crumble to the floor. I wanted to beg. Plead my case. Divert his attention. Make him stop. But something wouldn't let me. It could have been that look in his eye, on his face. It was probably pride.

"Fuck you," I said.

He took one step towards me. I tensed, then looked wildly around. The bathroom! I raced towards it, but he grabbed my middle and threw me to the floor. I screamed and swatted at him like a wild animal, but he was stronger than I was. And a lot more determined.

He grabbed my shirt and ripped it—and I mean literally ripped it—off my back. He did the same to my bra, to my short skirt, to my panties. Then I was naked, squirming beneath him crying and begging him to stop. The lesson had been learned! I knew then I would never be able to pull anything over on him. I had pushed him too far and I knew it. I was sorry I had tried.

"Please," I moaned. "Just please stop, Frank. I'll do whatever you want, just don't hit me!"

"Shut up. Please."

I tried to grab his face, I tried to kiss him, hoping that would soften him, that it would alter his direction, his path of destruction. It didn't. He pushed me off him and I fell backwards, the back of my head hitting the floor. My head swam, then began to throb. I think I blacked out. I couldn't be sure, but the next thing I know, he had me turned over and was beating me with the belt, like some sick motherfucker. He didn't just tap me, either, he belted me, lashed me at me. My body tensed and shivered with each lash. I quivered and wanted to beg him to stop, but I couldn't. I was in shock at his actions. *How long was he going to keep this up?*

I was finally able to cry, "What are you doing?"

"I'm breaking you."

I stopped moving, the terror of what he'd just said sank in and it sank in so hard I felt it land in my belly with a reverberating wallop.

Breaking me? Of what? From what? What was I? Some wild horse? Some wild animal? What the hell did that mean?!

I finally came back to my senses and was able to scream, "You're evil!"

He ignored me and gave me another lash. This time I felt sick, nauseous. I held my hand over my mouth to keep it in, but it didn't work. I threw up, gagging and coughing all over the floor.

He stopped.

I stared up at him, half-ashamed of what I'd just done, though it wasn't really my fault. I no longer felt the sting from the lashes, I felt the sting of embarrassment.

He eyed me for a moment, sighed, then went into the bathroom, returning with a towel. He threw it at me.

"Clean it up."

I sniffled and sat up. I wiped lamely at the vomit. He cursed, left for the bathroom again, came back with a few washcloths, then got on his hands and knees and started to help me.

"You know what your problem is," he said. "You don't know what's good for you."

My mouth fell open.

"It's true. You don't know what's good for you," he continued. "You test people. You like to see how far you can push people. But let me tell you one thing, I won't be pushed."

"I hate you."

He didn't bat an eye. But I could tell it bothered him.

I repeated, my words getting more and more intense as I spat them at him, "I hate you. I hate you! I HATE YOU!"

He grabbed me by the back of my head and pulled me up to him until our noses were touching. I wanted to slap him so badly then. Just one slap, right across his face.

"No you don't hate me. You hate yourself. You don't know what's good for you, Kristine. I am going to show you."

I shook my fists in the air and screamed at the top of my lungs, "I HATE YOU! I HATE YOU! I HATE YOU!"

He grabbed me again and this time he kissed me. A hard, lewd kiss. Slobbering. I fought against him, shoving at his hard body as best I could to get him away from me, but he kept at me, sticking his hot tongue in my mouth. I bit down hard on it. He pulled back, wiped his mouth with the back of his sleeve, stared at the blood on it, then smiled. It was almost as if he liked it.

Then he suddenly changed. Just like that. It was so strange. One moment he was irate, the next, he was apologetic. I dunno. I couldn't decipher it.

He was studying me then, looking almost remorseful. But it was like something had sparked his interest. I stared back, wondering what he was thinking. I couldn't bring myself to ask, though I was dying to know. But his attention was diverted. Having it diverted gave me time to jump up and run to the door. He sat back on his heels and watched me try to unlock it. I finally got it open and turned to him.

"Where are you going?" he asked softly.

"I'm leaving you!" I screamed and threw open the door.

"You don't have any clothes on," he said and nearly smiled.

I walked over to him and slapped him. He didn't flinch. He grabbed my arm and pulled me down to him. I struggled all the way down but his grip was tight and I couldn't squirm away from him.

"Where are you going to go, Kristine?" he asked, softly, staring into my eyes.

"As far away from you as possible."

He shook his head, telling me that, no, that wasn't going to happen. It infuriated me to have him do that to me.

"Let me go," I said, snarling. "Let me go."

He let me go. I was almost surprised. Almost a little disappointed. I didn't spend much time thinking about it, though. I looked around frantically, trying to locate my clothes. I saw them in a pile near the bed. I ran over and bent to pick them up. I shook my head at my shirt. I pulled it on. Only one button was intact. It would do. I buttoned it and turned to him.

"You shouldn't have done that to me, Frank."

He sighed like he knew this already. "Listen, Kristine—"

"I don't want to listen," I said, feeling tears slide down my face.

"Come on," he said. "Let's talk about this."

"Fuck you!" I screamed as the tears streamed down my face. "You're sick!"

He stood and held one hand out towards me, palm up, which terrified me even more.

"You better leave me alone," I said and pulled on my skirt.

"Kristine, come on," he said. "Let's talk about this."

"I don't want to talk!" I screamed at him.

"I'm sorry I lost my temper, but you—"

I pointed at him, "I didn't deserve that!"

He hung his head and nodded in agreement.

I wiped the tears off my face with the back of my hand and muttered, "You're mean."

"I'm sorry," he said, glancing up at me. "Tell me what I can do to remedy this."

"You can leave me alone," I said and stepped into my heels. "For good."

"You don't mean that."

"I do," I said, sobbing. "I really do."

My clothes on, I turned on my heel and ran from the room. He followed me, but he didn't run. I knew he wasn't about to let me go but I had to get out of there. Everything in my body told me to run, run, *RUN!*

I raced down the hall and was about to sprint down the stairs when he called out to me, "We need to talk about this!"

I turned to see him coming at me. In a panic, I took one step down, backwards. My ankle twisted as my heel caught on the first step. I cried out, then he rushed over to me, which made me panic, which made me lose my balance, which made me stumble and fall. Backwards.

"*KRISTINE!*"

Before I fell, I saw his face and then his hand, reaching out to save me. I grabbed for it desperately but it was too late and I fell backwards, my body doing a somersault along the stairs before I reached the bottom, where my head was the first thing to hit and it hit hard.

I didn't black out at first. My mind tried in vain to stay active and search out something to help me. I knew I was in trouble, I knew I was in a bad way, but I couldn't do anything about it. By the time he got to me, my head was spinning. No, my whole body was spinning, out of control. It was the worse feeling I'd ever had. Not only that, I was having trouble breathing. I coughed. I tried to cough. I couldn't cough! I couldn't breathe! I couldn't do anything but lay there and allow my body to convulse, to tremble, to shudder, to shake with panic.

My eyes closed. I blacked out. I don't know how long I laid there trembling, but all of a sudden I heard something. I couldn't tell what it was. I listened closely and then recognized the sound as his voice, calling to me from what seemed like under a thick blanket. Maybe he was in another room? I stopped concentrating on it and blacked out again, then it happened once more and it lured me out of my sleep, teased me, tickled me. I wanted to reach out to it, to hold it. To have it.

Far off, I heard his voice, coming at me as softly as a June wind, "Kristine?"

I tried to say something but I couldn't.

"Kristine?"

Uhhh…uh. No. I couldn't do it. I couldn't respond, though I wanted to, so badly. I wanted to reach out and touch him, but I couldn't move. It suddenly dawned on me that I couldn't move. I could not for the life of me move. Was this shock? Panic set in momentarily. What the fuck was happening to my body! TO ME!?

I felt something warm and wet on my face. He was washing my face, caressing it with a soft washcloth. It felt good against my face, warm, almost melodious, inviting. I could smell the fabric softener the maid used. It smelled like a baby, it was such a sweet smell. I blinked and opened my eyes.

"Kristine?" he said gently, with remorse.

I blinked and blinked, then was finally able to focus on him.

"Kristine?" he pleaded.

I managed to mutter, "Uhh…uh…"

He wiped my face tenderly, very much caressing it with the back of his hand. I tried to push it away. He wouldn't let me. He kept it there, then he turned me over, onto my stomach and I felt something red-hot on my back. I screamed and convulsed.

"Shh," he mumbled. "Shh. It's just alcohol. To clean the marks."

The marks? The marks. Oh, God. It all came back to me then, like a bad dream comes back at you once you're awake. I was suddenly frightened. I began to shake. I just knew he was going to beat me again.

I started to cry.

"Shh," he murmured and pressed his face against mine. "It's okay, baby."

"What are you doing?" I finally managed to cry.

"I'm just cleaning your back," he said.

He was tending my wounds? What the hell? Why was he doing this? I thought he wanted me dead.

"The doctor said you were lucky," he said and I heard him dip the washcloth into a bowl, squeeze out the excess water, then bring it to my face again. "You had a bad fall, but no broken bones. I thought for a minute that you were a goner."

I heard him sniffle, like he was trying to hold back tears. I listened, hanging on his every word.

"Your ankle was twisted, though, sprained," he said. "It's swollen, but it'll be okay in a few days."

My ankle? Then it all came back to me. All of it. The beating, then the fall. The panic.

I finally opened my eyes wide enough to look at him. His face was plastered with grief, an unbelievable look of grief. Some shame. He gently, oh so gently, wiped my back clean, then I felt momentary relief as he put some ointment on it, which felt cool. Then he rubbed it in and turned me back over.

I looked to the side. I was now in bed. I was lying on top of the silk comforter, bleeding onto it. I was naked. I stared at the window and was amazed to see daylight. How long had I been out?

"You'll be fine," he said softly and then the bastard began to brush my hair! My hair was wet! He'd given me a bath!

I tried my best to glare at him, but my face hurt so bad. And I had to pee.

I tried to speak. He bent over and pressed his ear next to my mouth. I whispered, "Pee."

"Oh!" he exclaimed and got up off the bed. "Can you walk?"

Could I walk? I finally managed to glare at him. *Why don't you tell me if I can walk?*

He stared back, then, without a word, bent over and scooped me up in his arms and carried me towards the bathroom. I couldn't do anything but try to hang on as best I could. Every step made my body ache like it had never ached before. I cried out several times and he shushed me gently.

He carried me all the way into the bathroom, then deposited me gently on the commode. When he let go, I almost fell over. He grabbed me just in time and held me up.

Then I urinated. I was almost embarrassed, but then I thought, *What does it matter?* Besides, I had been about to burst. I urinated for what seemed like years, then finally managed to open my eyes all the way, squinting at the bright light. I finally stopped peeing and sighed with relief as I looked around the marble bathroom, at the huge tub. I sighed. I stared at the marble floor then across at the vanity where I usually put on my make-up. Then at the mirror above the vanity. Terror caught in my throat and I almost screamed.

There—right there!—was some strange woman staring in the mirror at me. And she looked like hell. But, then…

No. Oh, no. NO NO *NO!*

It was no strange woman. It was me. Me! That was me! That woman, that person with the swollen eyes, so swollen they were almost shut, that woman was me! That fragile, beaten to death woman was me! I couldn't get over it. I'd be disfigured. How many times had the bastard hit me in the face? HOW MANY TIMES!

I got up and tried to approach the mirror to get a better look. I almost fell to the floor.

"Easy there," he said softly and held me up.

I ignored him and tried to get to the mirror to see myself. He held me tight. I pointed and he walked me over. When I saw what I looked like, I screamed at the top of my lungs. I screamed and I screamed and I screamed until I couldn't scream anymore, until I became hoarse. Then I screamed more and more until he covered my mouth with his hand and silenced me. Then I stared into the mirror, fully realizing how bad it was.

I was covered not only in bruises, but also in welts. All over my legs, my arms, my back, my stomach.

Oh, dear Lord! I looked like I had been run over by a truck, then they'd came back and run over me again, just to make sure they got me.

I wanted to kill him then. To beat him as he had beat me. I tried to swat at him, but I was too weak.

"I'm going to kill you!" I cried.

"Shh," he said and held me tight.

"How many times did you hit me in the face?" I asked and turned back to the mirror.

He shook his head. "That's from the fall."

The fall did this? I vaguely remember feeling the rough, wool carpet on my face. I stared at the welts. They were only a few of them, mostly on my back. All the rest was carpet burns. Rough, ugly, red scratchy scrapes all over my body.

But my face…Oh, dear God. My face was in shambles. It was swollen and looked so bad. It looked so bad it made me want to cry.

"When you fell…" he began, then cleared his throat. "You landed on your face."

I did? I stared back at myself in the mirror. Would it ever heal? Ever? I started sobbing and wanted to hit him so bad then. I turned and punched at him, but he ignored my sobs and my futile punches and lifted me back into his arms. He carried me into the bedroom, laid me down gently and kissed my forehead with his cool lips.

"You'll feel better soon," he said.

No, I felt like saying, I won't.

Instead, I said, "This is all your fault."

He nodded. "I know."

I despise him, I hate him, I love him.

Days passed. Not that I could do a damn thing about it. All I could do was lie there in that bed in a pain induced haze and stare dumbly up at the ceiling. I formulated a defense and plotted Frank's murder. Then I tried to reason for him, to understand why he did what he did. I couldn't think of any good reason, other than the fact that he was nuts. And he had to be nuts. Right?

He had said, "I'm breaking you."

What kind of sick motherfucker says something like that? Breaking me of what? From what? And why?

Unfortunately, he stayed by my side the majority of the time. He cleaned my wounds, spoon fed me, gave me painkillers and wouldn't let anyone in to see me. He did all of this gently as a mother. He even seemed to like doing it.

In about a week's time, I felt better. Not that I could run a marathon or anything, but I did feel better. My face was healing, too, which made me feel better. It didn't look like I was going to need any reconstructive surgery. Frank moved a TV into the bedroom and flipped channels for me, stopping when I would point at something I wanted to watch. And I made him sit through chick movies, soap operas and music videos.

He didn't say a word. He didn't say how sorry he was. He would just lean over and plant a kiss on my cheek ever so often. I just rolled my eyes and counted the minutes until I could smash something heavy over his head. Maybe a lamp? A small sculpture? A broom? What would be good?

Then, he'd plant another kiss on my cheek and I'd start the reasoning for him all over again. Trying to justify his actions so that I could understand what drove him to do something like this.

But he hadn't pushed me down the stairs…No. But I *had* been running away from him and that's why I fell. Because of him. It was his fault. The bastard.

One day he leaned over and planted a kiss on my cheek and before he pulled away, he said, "I love you."

I glared at him. He smiled back.

"I do," he said, almost happily. "I love you."

"*You love me?*"

He nodded and gave me another kiss. "Yes. I do."

I moved away from him, fuming. But I couldn't help myself. I had to ask, "So, if you love me, how could you beat me like that?"

He dropped his head. "Kristine, I'm sorry. I can't ever make what I did right, but I am sorry."

"But why did you do it?"

"I was extremely pissed off at you, that's why," he said. "I beat you because you did something you shouldn't have done. In my state of mind at the time, you deserved it."

"How do you justify it, though? How *can* you justify it?"

"I can't."

"That's what I thought."

"Listen," he said. "Most of your wounds are from the fall—"

"I fell because I thought you were going to kill me!"

"If I wanted to kill you, you'd be dead."

"That's really reassuring."

He nodded as if I'd given him a compliment. He had to be nuts. But what did that make me? I was the nut who put up with it. Why wasn't I gone from here? What was I waiting on? I had plenty of opportunity to leave. I could sneak out anytime I wanted to. Besides, I wasn't a prisoner, not that I knew of. I did have some free will. Some.

"So, you see," he said. "It's all for the best. Now we know where we stand."

"And where do we stand?" I asked, eying him.

"You know where," he said. "You know now not to pull that kind of shit you pulled."

"Whatever."

"You're not a teenager, you know."

"So?" I snapped. "And light me a cigarette."

He lit my cigarette and handed it to me, then said, "I'm just saying you're a little old to throw those kinds of parties."

I could have slapped him. Since when was thirty-two *old*? That was old? Well, if I was old, he was ancient. He was thirty-five.

"Please!" I said and took a drag. "What kind of parties should I throw? Ones where all the people come dressed in dinner gowns and tuxes?"

"Or at the very least, the people should be dressed."

We stared at each other for a moment, then we couldn't help it. We cracked up.

He grinned. "I saw some of those women and I thought I was in a stripclub."

"You met me in a stripclub."

"I know."

"Why did you, of all people, come into my stripclub?"

"I met someone there. A business associate who likes those kinds of clubs."

"And you don't like them?"

"Oh, I didn't say that, Kristine," he said and leaned back on the bed, hands behind his head. "I like stripclubs but I don't have a lot of time to go to them."

I eyed him.

"I don't look down on those people as much as you think I do. In fact, I think strippers are very enterprising."

"Whatever," I said and took a drag. "Why did you keep coming back?"

"Because of you, obviously."

I hid my smile. I knew that, but it was good to hear.

"I mean, you floored me," he said.

Yeah, I knew it.

He smiled and kissed my cheek. "I had to have you."

"You could have been nicer, though."

"Oh, right," he said. "And have you walk all over me?"

I sat up and pointed at him with my cigarette. "That's what this is all about, isn't it? Me walking all over you and you can't stand it!"

He looked away towards the window.

"Frank?"

"What?" he said, still staring at the window.

"Is that why you did it? Are you afraid I'll walk all over you?"

He nodded. "Yes. Let's not talk about this."

"Why? Does it make you uncomfortable?"

"Yes," he muttered. "It does. Please let it drop."

I let it drop and smoked my cigarette, dropping the ash into the ashtray he held for me.

"I just wanted you to know, that's all," he muttered.

"Know what?"

"Know that I love you."

"Well, I hate you."

"No, you don't."

"Yes. I do."

"Kristine," he said, moving closer to me. "Right now you feel humbled. You feel frightened. You feel—"

"Stop telling me how I feel, you asshole! I feel hatred towards you right now because you beat me! I feel anxious that you'll do it again!"

"I won't do it again, Kristine," he said, staring into my eyes. "Not unless you give me reason."

"Oh, and that was reason enough to beat someone? Throwing a party?"

"You did so without my knowledge, without my permission. You didn't even invite me."

"Invite you! Why would I invite *you?* You weren't even in town!"

"That hurt, too," he said.

"That's not enough reason to beat me," I said. "Besides, I only invited thirty people, but more came. It wasn't my fault they all showed up."

He sighed. "Oh."

"So really you had no right to do that to me. It wasn't my fault."

"Still, though, a lot of antiques were damaged and—"

"Who cares if one of your stupid chairs gets a scratch? It's just stuff."

"That's not the point."

"What is the point?"

He sighed. "The point is, you didn't even consider me when you planned all this. You were only thinking of yourself."

That wasn't entirely true.

"You keep me locked away here," I said. "I had to have some contact with the outside world."

"Then why not throw a party in a bar?" he asked.

I snorted and looked away.

"And why stay, Kristine?" he asked softly, touching my am. "If you hate me, why not leave?"

"Why should I leave?" I asked. "Why don't you leave? Why don't you break up with me so I *can* leave?"

"I don't want you to, that's why and you know it."

I sighed, "You didn't have to call the cops."

"I didn't. The neighbors did."

I stared at him. He wasn't lying. I could tell that. Well, it made sense. I vaguely remembered a policeman at the front door, telling me to wind it down soon, me promising and then inviting him in for a drink. Him coming in and getting lost in the crowd.

Well, I'll be damned.

I stared at the TV, which was turned off. He gave me a little kiss on my cheek. Then he turned my head towards his and grazed his lips against mine. Softly. Softly enough to send shivers up and down my spine. Softly enough for me to want more where that came from.

He kissed me then, kissed me gently, passionately. Wide open kissed me, all of me, my being. I couldn't stop. I wanted to stop. I couldn't have stopped if my life depended on it. I turned to him and took his face between my hands and pulled him to me, pulled his body on top of mine, helped him undress, helped his hard cock into my body. And he made love to me. We'd never made love before. We'd only fucked. Now we were making love. He caressed my body, he didn't devour it as he did before. He kissed me, stroked me. Brought me to one intense orgasm and then another. An orgasm that was tender and sweet and belonged in my body. Belonged to him. Just like I did.

After it was over, he told me again that he loved me. And he waited. He waited a long time. He was right. I didn't hate him. Even after all that, I couldn't. My body, my soul and my heart craved him too much for hatred to dominate my feelings.

"I love you, too," I said, realizing it was easy to say, that I wanted to say it, that I felt it. That it scared me to open myself up like that. That I wanted to hide it, to take it back, but knowing I couldn't.

"See?" he said, satisfied. "You don't hate me. I knew you didn't."

He was right. And with that, I inched a little closer to being completely and utterly under his control, to losing myself in him. To losing everything that I had become and would become to him, to this man. To his love. To his prison.

But I wasn't about to let him break me. I still had too much pride for that.

Sprained ankle.

I was up in about a week. My face was healing and it didn't look like it was going to scar. My body was still sore from the fall, but the painkillers made it all easier to deal with.

I knew I looked like shit. I refused to go out anywhere and asked Frank to give all the house staff a week or so off. I didn't want anyone to see me like this.

My sprained ankle hurt like a motherfucker. It took me forever to learn how to walk on the crutches. First you have to put them under your arms, hold the hurt foot up (or out, whichever you prefer) and balance. That's the easy part. Then you have to maneuver the crutches by lifting them at the same time to propel your body forward. By the time I learned to get around on them, I could walk without their assistance.

But before that happened, something strange happened.

One day I thought I was home alone and was walking around on the crutches and by this time I was getting around on them pretty good. I was downstairs in the living room and decided to go into the kitchen and get some tea. I got up and made my way in there. But then I thought I'd also like a sandwich. I was reading a really good book and wanted to read while I ate. So, I turned around and went back into the living room, grabbed the book, shoved it under my arm, then went back out into the hall.

As I hobbled, the book fell out from under my arm.

"Shit," I said and bent over to pick it up. But I lost my balance and fell flat on my ass and my foot went behind and twisted. Again. The crutches fell noisily beside me.

I cried out in pain and started to cuss.

"Motherfucking hell!" I cried as tears began to stream down my face. It hurt like absolute hell. It was a sharp pain, way down deep in the bone. I felt it in my nerves, too. It was a taunting, deep pain.

I sat there for a few minutes and cried like a baby. And that's what I felt like, a baby who needed its rest and food and sleep. I needed someone to help me then, to help me up, to give me a painkiller. I just needed someone because I couldn't move.

I suddenly got the feeling that I wasn't alone.

I looked up and my eyes were met directly with Frank's. He was staring at me, mesmerized. I stared back and wondered what the hell he was doing. He didn't move. He was transfixed by something. I wanted to say something, to call out to him, but I was almost afraid to break the spell.

I didn't have to say anything. In a second flat, he sprinted over towards me. He bent to my eye level and stared into my eyes,

"Does it hurt much?" he asked softly, but with an intensity that was a little peculiar.

I shrugged and wiped my face off with the back of my hand, "Not always, but now it does. I twisted it again."

He stared at me. "I'm sorry, baby."

"I know, Frank, you tell me everyday."

"No, I mean I'm sorry it hurts."

I stared at him. What the hell was he getting at?

"Me, too," I said a little uneasily.

"Would you like me to rub it?" he asked.

I stared at him.

"Would that make it feel better?"

"Maybe," I said.

He sat down and motioned for me to give him my foot. I stretched my leg out, laid it in his lap and he took my foot between his hands and began to rub it, ever so gently.

"It's all swollen," he said and stared at my ankle.

I stared at it, too and nodded. "Yup."

He continued to rub it, holding it in both hands. He rubbed it like a nurse would, carefully. But then he rubbed a little too hard.

I gasped and said, "Shit! Watch it!"

He stopped and stared at me. "I'm sorry. I didn't mean to do that."

I sighed and sat back. "It's okay. Just be careful."

He nodded quietly and began to rub then he stopped and stared at me. "Can I take your bandage off?"

"Why?"

"I dunno. I just want to see your ankle."

God, he's so weird, I thought, but I nodded anyway.

"Sure, go ahead, but be careful."

He grinned and took off the clasps, set them to the side, then began to unravel the bandage.

"You have to put it back on, though," I said as he unraveled the last of it.

"I will."

"I know you will."

He held my foot in his hand and stared at it. I stared, too. It was swollen and black and blue. It looked awful.

He bent and kissed it. I smiled. Then he pressed his face against it.

"What are you doing?"

He shrugged and smiled at me. "Nothing."

I chuckled, "You are doing something, Frank. Tell me."

"No," he said and began to lick my ankle, all over the sore spot. I sighed. Ahh, that felt so good.

"Like that?" he asked.

I bit my lip and nodded. "Yeah."

He began to caress it again. I began to feel it. I began to get wet, juicy. Just by his touch, which was so gentle and caring. I moaned.

That was his indicator. He stopped rubbing and set my foot on the floor gently, parted my legs and bent over me. I arched and met his lips. He began to kiss me then, kiss me differently. It was a slow, amorous kiss. His mouth was open wide, then he'd shut it, like he was eating my mouth. I matched his kiss and did the same, which elicited a deep moan from him.

He pushed me back on the floor and tugged my shirt up, then dove between my legs, eating at my crotch through my shorts. I moaned and grabbed his head, tugging at him, letting him know he could take the rest of my clothes off. His hand unzipped my shorts and he pulled them down my legs, threw them over his shoulder and came back up the inside of my leg using his tongue.

By this time I was so wet, I slid around on the floor.

I grabbed at his zipper and pulled it down. He helped, pulled his dick out and put it in. Then he fucked me. I sighed with relief. For a while now, we'd been making love, which was great, but fucking is what I like best. I liked the way his dick filled me, then thrust into me.

"Ahh, yeah," I said and bit at his ear. "Fuck me, baby."

He did so and gave a thrust that made me scream. He took my leg and held it up, so he got in deeper. I liked that. I told him so. He grinned back at me and kissed me again, then bent and bit at my nipple, which made me rise off the floor and meet him thrust for thrust.

"I'm gonna come," he moaned and buried his face in my neck, which he ate at like a vampire.

I held his head and grunted, "So am I."

And I was. I was coming fast and hard, being so turned on I couldn't contain myself. And it was a deep, intense one. So intense I grabbed out for him and scratched his chest.

"Ahh!" he yelled, obviously in pain.

"I'm sorry," I breathed but didn't stop.

He didn't stop, either. We couldn't have stopped no matter what. We were like two wild animals on the floor fucking like we were supposed to fuck and when we came, we both cried out in pain.

It was that powerful.

He fell away from me, panting. I laid there panting. We didn't move for a while. I noticed we were both sweating profusely. I leaned over and wiped his brow. Just as I was about to take my hand away, he grabbed it and put it around his dick. I complied and moved my hand up and down it, then bent and put it in my mouth. Even though it was rapidly deflating, it was still hard. And as I sucked, he came again, came right into my mouth, his sperm. Not a lot of it, but some.

He grabbed the back of my head and held onto it, held me there and he let out a loud cry as if it were the best thing he'd ever felt, but it hurt a little too.

I stared at him. He stared back. We couldn't believe he'd just done that. Neither one of us. He grinned sheepishly and opened his arms. I laid down on his chest and he kissed the top of my head.

"Do you just come again?" I asked.

He nodded and cleared his throat. "I guess maybe I didn't get it all out the first time."

"I've never seen anything like that."

"I've never done anything like that."

I sighed. "You were horny, weren't you?"

"Yes, I was."

"Why were you so horny? We just had sex this morning."

"Why do you always ask these stupid questions? I'm always horny for you, you know that."

I grinned. I did know it, but it felt good to hear, too.

"Thanks for rubbing my ankle," I said, then laughed. "Why did you do that?"

He shrugged.

I sat up on my elbow and stared him down. "Tell me."

He said, "I don't know what came over me, but when I saw you like that, all weak and helpless, it just drove me crazy."

"Really?"

He nodded.

"Did it turn you on?"

"Yes, it did. Tremendously."

"Wow," was all I could think of to say. "What else turns you on?"

He smiled, but didn't reply. I was about to find out.

Honey.

After the sprained ankle incident, things began to change in our relationship. All relationships are about sex to a certain degree, but ours became about games. And that's what started the games. That's where the door cracked, then swung wide open.

It all started innocently enough. I guess it was just a natural progression in our relationship. They were fun games, silly even. They made us laugh and smile. The day after a game was played, I'd sit and think about it and just crack up. They were that fun.

Just after I was done with the crutches, the phone rang about ten in the morning. It was a Wednesday.

"Hello?"

"Kristine," he said, calling from work, or whatever the hell he called it.

"*Franklin.*"

"Kristine," he said. "I've given Pierre and cook the day off."

"Ohhh…kay."

"What are you going to do?"

"Going to do?" I asked and glanced around the living room. "Just watch some TV or—"

"No," he said, silencing me. "What are you going to do for supper?"

"Oh!" I exclaimed and thought about it. "I could order in or maybe we could—"

"No," he said, again silencing me. "You will not. You will cook supper for us tonight."

I wasn't so convinced. Cook? For him? There was no way. I made a mean spaghetti and meatballs, but he wasn't the spaghetti and meatballs kinda guy. He ate veal that had little green things sprinkled all over it. He ate things I couldn't pronounce. He ate things I didn't like to eat because I didn't like fancy food. I was too meat and potatoes for escargot or any of that other fancy crap. Besides, I wasn't going to eat snails even if they did give them a fancy crème sauce and a fancy name to go along with them. Uh huh. No.

He cut into my thoughts, "I have prepared a menu."

"Tonight?" I asked hesitantly. "You want me to cook tonight?"

"Yes, Kristine," he said, losing patience. "You will cook for us tonight."

"I will?"

"Yes!"

I still wasn't convinced.

"Kristine," he said in that warning voice. "Listen to me. I have prepared a menu, which I will fax to the house."

"If you say so," I said and stifled a yawn.

"You will receive it shortly," he said and hung up.

I stared at the receiver, then set the phone down. Not a minute later, the fax machine on the desk was spitting out a menu. I grabbed it.

Menu: Pot roast, mashed potatoes, green beans, rolls, lime jello.

Lime jello?

Well, that was certainly an All-American meal. I smiled. I could do this in no time. He must have guessed I couldn't cook anything fancy.

I rushed to the grocery store, bought up the items, rushed back and found a crock-pot in the cabinet. I prepared the pot roast, stuck it in there and started peeling the potatoes. I worked my ass off until about two that afternoon, only stopping once to light a cigarette, which dangled from my lips as I chopped vegetables.

I could be a short order cook. I'd be a good one. I giggled at the thought.

He called around four. "I will be home at six. I expect supper to be on the table."

Then I suddenly got it! He was acting like a man. A man with a woman at home, who stayed home, who cooked for him, who took care of him.

He continued, "I have purchased you a dress, which will arrive at the house shortly. Please put it on, with the stockings and the heels."

"Yes, sir," I teased.

He growled, "Don't 'yes, sir', me."

"Uh, sorry. Sir."

"Kristine," he said. "I am your husband. You don't have to call me sir."

My husband? Well, well, well. And I didn't even remember the wedding.

"Can I call you master then?" I teased, twirling the phone cord around my fingers. "Please, master."

"No," he said. "You can only refer to me tonight as 'honey.'"

"'Honey'?"

"Yes. 'Honey.'"

"Okay, honey."

The doorbell rang.

"Go get that," he ordered. "That will be your dress."

"Bye!" I squealed and hung up before he could respond. I ran to the door, threw it open and a tall, elegantly dressed woman jerked back.

"Oh, sorry," she drawled. "Are you Kristine?"

"Yes, that's me."

"I'm Liddy," she said and patted a thin dress box. "This is for you."

88   Breaking the Girl

I reached out for it. She held it back.

"No, sweetie," she said, smiling as if she were embarrassed for me. "I have to make sure it fits."

"Oh," I said. "Okay."

I lead her into the living room. She sat on the sofa and placed the box in her lap, like she was protecting it. She smiled. I smiled back and waited for her to let me have it.

"You'll need to try it on, of course," she said and laid the box on the couch, then opened it delicately.

I stood back and watched her, thinking she must have some prize in there. I was astounded when she pulled out a rather plain, but pretty dress. Kind of like the ones Mrs. Cleaver would have worn on *Leave it to Beaver*.

She held it up and smiled at me. "Please be careful. This is on loan."

I had to ask, "What is so great about this dress?"

She gasped. "It's vintage, sweetie!"

"Oh."

She nodded. "Your husband wanted it, but I couldn't part with it, so we worked something out so you could wear it tonight."

I didn't bother telling her Frank was not my husband. Or that that this was all a game.

I nodded at her and held my hand out for the dress. She shooed my hand away and stood.

"Just undress and we'll make sure it fits."

Being a former stripper, I didn't mind this. The only thing that bothered me was a prominent bite mark on my ass that my "husband" had given me the previous night. But I had panties covering my ass, so she might not see it.

After I was undressed, she held the dress out and I stepped into it. It fit like a glove, which meant I could barely breathe in it. It also smelled musty and the old cotton was rougher than any material I'd ever worn. But once I turned and looked in the mirror, I grinned. I looked like a hot fifties housewife.

She bent this way and that, tugging at the dress, then she sighed, "Well, you don't need any alterations. It fits perfectly."

I nodded and twirled around. "I love it!"

She smiled and touched my arm. "Please, be careful. This is a one of a kind and I have it displayed in my shop."

"Which shop?" I asked.

"Tree Jordan's," she said. "On Magazine."

I didn't know it, but I nodded like I did.

She reached back into the box and pulled out vintage heels, an apron and a set of pearls. Then silk stockings, a garter belt and a girdle! I'd never worn a girdle in my entire life.

"Now," she said. "With a little make-up and hair, you'll be the perfect housewife."

I stared at myself. "Yeah, I guess you're right."

"Well, that about does it," she said and tried to smile. I could tell she was having a hard time letting this dress go.

"I'll be extra careful with it," I promised.

She nodded and actually wiped at her eye, like she was about to cry.

"Please do," she mumbled, then let herself out.

"Poor thing," I muttered after I heard the front door close. I glanced at the clock. It was five. I barely had enough time to finish up the meal and to get some make-up on.

I rushed around like a chicken with its head cut off, and was seated in the "parlor" with a cigarette (in cigarette holder) when I heard him come in. I tensed with anticipation.

He walked in, ignored me, threw his briefcase down, and plopped in the chair opposite me.

"Hey," he muttered.

"Hey yourself," I said, unsure of where this was leading.

"Where's my drink?" he asked.

"Oh!" I said and jumped up. I smiled at him before racing over to the bar where I fixed him his favorite martini (vodka with an olive). I slowly walked back towards him, swinging my hips. I bent down, delivered the martini and stood back up.

"Thanks," he muttered. "What's for dinner? I'm starving."

"Pot roast," I said and sat down in his lap. "With creamed potatoes and—"

"Good," he said and pushed me out of his lap. "Let's eat."

I watched in amazement as he left the room headed for the dining room. Well, alright then. I got up and followed him. He was already seated when I walked in the dining room.

"Smells good," he mumbled then opened a newspaper and flicked it so the pages would smooth out.

I stared at him. He stared back, over the newspaper.

"Well?" he asked.

"Aren't you even going to say anything?"

"About what?"

"About anything!" I half-yelled, really getting into my role as the over-looked wife. "Look at this meal! At me!"

He eyed me, the meal. He nodded.

"Good job, honey."

I stared at him. Well, he had told me I'd done a good job. I decided to go with it.

"Thanks. Honey."

"Am I going to have to beg for it?" He asked.

I sighed loudly as if I were *this* close to telling him to fuck off, then fixed him a plate, plopping the food down onto it. I shoved it under his newspaper, then sat down, crossed my arms and glared at him.

He didn't take notice. I almost smiled. He was really playing it up, too. He started to eat, while reading the paper, just like I wasn't even in the room.

He glanced over at me. "Aren't you going to eat?"

"Oh! Yeah, I almost forgot," I said and prepared myself a plate.

He shrugged and gobbled down everything on his plate. Then he looked around. "Where's my beer?"

"Your *beer*?"

He nodded. "Yeah. You know I like a beer with pot roast."

"Oh, sorry," I said. "I've had so much on my mind lately. I'll get it."

I hopped up and raced into the kitchen, where I located a six pack in the fridge. I grabbed one, then a glass and raced to the door. I stopped at the door, pushed it open with my hip, and sauntered in, really swinging my hips as I walked over to him. He didn't notice, so I stopped about half-way there and walked like I usually do.

He glanced up at me and winked.

I smiled and put the swing back into my hips and made my way over, stopping at the table. I bent over and poured the beer while he stared at me from the corner of his eye.

"There you go, honey," I said sweetly.

He nodded, sipped the beer, then he held out his plate to me.

"Yes?" I asked.

"May I have some more pot roast? Please?"

I grabbed the plate and loaded food onto it. I plopped it back down in front of him, then I picked up my fork and moved my food around a little, staring at him from the corner of my eye.

He folded the newspaper, grabbed the plate, hunched over it and ate it like a truck driver. Or a coal miner. He didn't even pause to wipe his mouth. I watched him, mouth agape. Then he leaned back and gave a big burp. I cringed.

"Would you like some more?" I asked.

"No, thanks," he said, eying my plate. "Aren't you hungry?"

"No. I had a big lunch."

"Oh," he said. "Then you can clear the dishes."

"Of course."

"And bring me another beer."

"Sure, honey." I said began to clear the dishes.

"Be sure to wear latex gloves when you wash the dishes," he called as I carried them into the kitchen. "You don't want to ruin your manicure."

I stared down at my nails. He was right.

I smiled at him, kicked the door open with my foot, walked over to the sink and threw the dishes down. One of the plates broke in half. Shit! Oh, well. What did it matter? I went back in, gathered the remaining dishes and smiled at him. He didn't smile back. He now had his feet propped up on the table and was leaned back, smoking a cigarette and sipping his beer. I bent over in front of him to grab his plate and his hand came down and slapped me right across the ass. It stung like hell.

I jerked up and whirled around. "What the hell was that for?"

"An ass like that," he said, grinning. "Deserves a good slapping."

He slapped it again, this time squeezing it with his hand.

"Watch it," I said, going back into the kitchen. "Honey."

I washed the dishes in about ten minutes. Then I went back into the dining room. He was still in the same position, only his cigarette was extinguished. He eyed me.

"Honey," he said. "I want you to get up on the table now."

"Excuse me?"

"Get up on the table."

"For what?"

"I want to see what's under that dress."

I began to tense with anticipation. I did as I was told. I slid up on to the table and crossed my legs.

"No," he said. "On all fours."

I got up on all fours.

He grabbed my legs and pulled them apart and peered between them. I almost cracked up. What was he doing? Giving me an exam?

He sighed and I felt his warm breath on my legs. I felt myself getting warm, growing moist. He did that to me. He could just look at me and I'd be ready.

He laughed. "What the hell is that thing you're wearing?"

I stared back at him from over my shoulder. "It's a girdle. It completes the authentic look."

He shook his head, still eying the girdle. Then he reached between my legs and began to tug it off. I wriggled so he could get it down. He threw it over his shoulder.

"That's the ugliest thing I've ever seen," he muttered.

I giggled. It was ugly as hell.

His hand went up between my ass cheeks sideways, then down. He stopped to finger me. I was now dripping.

He slapped my ass again like I was a piece of meat. I wiggled and stared back at him. He didn't return my gaze. He just kept looking at my ass like it was the first time he'd seen it. Then he ran his hand up my leg, holding it, squeezing it.

"I like your stockings," he said. "And I see you have a garter belt on."

"Yes, honey."

"The dress is nice, too," he said. "Did you get it on sale?"

I smiled, playing along. "No. It was full price. Is that okay, honey? That I paid full price? We can afford it, can't we?"

He shrugged. "This time, but you're going to have to stop your damn spending!"

I hid my smile and said very seriously, "I'll do better next time. I promise."

He was now fingering my clit, stroking it, bringing it and me under his control. I moaned and spread my legs wider.

"Honey," I moaned. "Climb up here and fuck me."

He only response was another hard slap to my ass, then a grunt, like he liked doing that, slapping my ass. I know I liked it. He squeezed it again.

"You're fucking the neighbor, aren't you?" he asked suddenly.

I tensed. "No."

"Don't lie to me," he growled. "I saw you."

"No, no," I said, playing along, pretending to be in a panic. "You didn't see me. I only fuck you."

"Don't lie to me, bitch," he said and I heard him pull his zipper down. "Is his cock as big as mine?"

He pushed it between my ass cheeks, running it up and down. It slid along happily, getting lost in my juice. I moaned.

"No," I murmured. "Your cock is much, much bigger."

"Then why are you fucking him?" he growled and pulled my head back. He began to lick and kiss my neck, suckle it.

"I just did," I moaned. "I don't know why!"

"Yes, you do," he said. "You did it because you're a little slut. Isn't that right?"

He gave another jerk to my head. I moaned with ecstasy.

"NO!" I cried. "I did it cause you work all the time! You don't pay any attention to me! You don't love me!"

"Love you?" he hissed and let my head fall. "How could I love a woman who sticks another man's cock in her mouth?"

"I didn't do that with him," I moaned. "I only let him fuck me."

He leaned over and whispered, "Where did you let him fuck you?"

"Just up the ass," I whispered. "I told him my cunt belonged to you."

He laughed harshly. I knew he'd like that one.

"Come on, baby," I said. "Stick it in my pussy, your pussy, it belongs to you. I'd never let another man touch it."

He did as he was told. He stuck it in my cunt then, filling me up with every single inch of his hard cock. He took me like a bitch. Fucked me like a bitch. I couldn't get enough. I wanted it all, then some more. More, more, more.

"Besides," I moaned. "You're fucking your secretary."

"So what?" he said. "She doesn't give me shit and she works cheap."

"She's a whore!" I screamed. "She sucks your cock every day before you come home! There's nothing left for me!"

"I got plenty for the both of you," he said and leaned over and kissed my neck, then bit at my ear. "Then some."

"But I want it all," I said and moaned. "It's mine. Your cock belongs to me."

"No, it doesn't," he said. "I can fuck any bitch I want with it."

He accented the last syllable with a hard thrust. I gasped. Then he grabbed the front of my dress, yanked it, and, consequently, tore it apart. It fell off me in pieces. I stared down at it. Oh fucking shit!

"Oh shit!" I yelled. "She'll kill me!"

He was fucking me, not missing a beat as he asked, "Who?"

"Liddy! The dress woman! She said this was on loan!"

Oh, God I'd never be able to fix it! I almost stopped him, but of course, I didn't. Fuck the dress for now. There wasn't anything I could do about it. I'd worry about it after we were done.

"Fuck Liddy," he muttered.

Yeah, fuck her.

"Oh, honey," I moaned. "Fuck *me* harder. You like giving it to me, don't you?"

"Uh huh," he said and complied, driving his cock deep inside me. I pushed back against him, which pressed it in deeper and deeper.

He grabbed me by the hair of the head and pulled my face to his. He hissed, "I don't like it when you fuck around on me."

"I won't do it again," I said and begged, "Please, fuck me harder."

He gave another push. I gasped.

"You should pay for what you did."

"I won't do it again! I promise!"

"I think you need a spanking," he said.

"Noooo!" I wailed as he pulled out. "Don't!"

But he had me turned over and pulled off the table, and I was bent across his lap, my bare ass sticking in the air.

"I'm going to spank you now," he said and reared back. His hand landed on my bare ass with a resounding *WHACK!*

I screamed, "NO!"

"I'll show you to fuck around on me," he said and gave me another whack, then another, and another until I was writhing in his lap, until I was squirming, coming, coming so hard I nearly fell to the floor. I wanted my hand—or his hand—on my pussy so bad then. I put mine there, but he pulled it back, held my arm tight and wouldn't let me touch myself.

"Please," I begged. "Please let me touch it!"

"No," he said and gave me another good whack, so hard this time I nearly jumped out of my skin and ran away.

"Please," I begged and tried to get my arm back. "Let me rub it a little."

"No."

Another whack.

"OH GOD!" I screamed. "PLEASE FUCK ME NOW!"

He grabbed me by the hair again and hissed, "Promise me you won't fuck him again!"

"I won't fuck him again! I promise!"

He seemed pleased with my answer. I almost smiled gratefully at him.

He gave me one last whack, then bent and kissed my now red ass, picked me up, sat me on the table, then spread my legs and dove in, sucking and eating at my pussy, getting lost in there like I was lost in him. I grabbed him by the hair of the head and held him still as I wrapped my legs around his head and humped his face. Humped him until I came and came and then came again. I screamed as I came, screamed his name with all my might.

"Now fuck me," I said.

He got up, stuck it in and fucked me, pushing me back on the table, pushing me down and overcoming me with his cock. I grabbed onto his ass and pushed him deep inside and I didn't let go until I came again. Until he came. Until it was over. And when it was over, we fell away from each other gasping for air.

He glanced at me and said, "You're a good fuck, Kristine, but you can't cook for shit."

I didn't reply. He was right.

Maid for a day.

The next time:

"I will be home in one hour," he said.

I smiled and stared at the clock. One hour away was six o'clock.

"The maid is off this week."

"Yes?" I said and smiled.

"You will need to scrub the kitchen floor," he said. "When I come home, you will be down on your hands and knees scrubbing the floor. You will wear the maid's uniform that I put in your closet yesterday."

"When did you do that?"

"Kristine," he sighed. "Just put it on. Oh, no panties. Got it?"

I nodded. "Yes, got it."

"Also, do not clean the floor with ammonia. It will strip the wax. Use oil soap."

"Okay."

He hung up.

I raced upstairs and found the maid's uniform stuck in the very back of the closet in a garment back. I grinned. It was a French maid's uniform. A little black uniform that consisted of a short little skirt with ruffles and a plunging neckline.

I put it on, then a garter, stocking and, lastly, a pair of black pumps. No panties, of course. I put my hair up, pulled strands down in my face, then I went all out on my make-up.

Damn. I looked hot.

I found a bucket, a sponge and the oil soap. I checked the clock. He'd be home in ten minutes. I filled the bucket with water and got down on all fours, pointing my ass at the door. And I waited.

In ten minutes he was home, slamming the front door. He came directly into the kitchen. I scrubbed the floor and ignored him. He stood in the doorway and watched me. I moved my ass a little as I scrubbed and hummed like I was alone. He didn't move from the doorway for a long time. I could tell he was devouring me with his eyes. He liked to watch.

I sighed and sat up, then dipped the sponge in the water. I squeezed it out all over my white shirt, until it was drenched and my nipples were visible and poking through.

I got back to work, moving backwards towards the door. Towards him.

He still didn't move.

I kept cleaning and moving backwards, until I felt his foot. He lifted my skirt with it and looked in. Then he bent, cupped my ass, running his hands up and down my bare skin, sending goosebumps all over my body.

I shivered and continued to clean. He continued to paw at me.

"How long have you been a maid?" he asked.

"All my life," I said, not looking at him.

"Do you enjoy your work?" he asked, pushing a finger into my pussy.

I stiffened. "Sir, please. I don't know you."

"Yes, you do," he said and bent down. His tongue flicked out and grazed my lips, spreading them. "You've been my maid for a long time."

"Sir, please," I begged. "Please don't make me."

"But your pussy is so sweet," he said and began to really kiss it. "You've always wanted me. I can see it in your eyes. I can see it when you stare at me from across the room. I've always known it."

"But what about your wife?" I asked.

"She's not here. Don't worry about her."

He put two fingers in me. It felt so good, I nearly jumped from the floor. Then he moved them around.

"You're so wet," he muttered. "You're so wet for me."

"Yes."

"We'll do this," he muttered. "Then we'll pretend it never happened."

"Oh, sir, no, please, I can't!"

I pretended to try to get away, but he held me tight, grabbing me by the waist. He turned me over, tore open my shirt and devoured my breasts, squeezing one with one hand while the other one was in my pussy. I moaned and raised my hips off the floor. He pulled his hand out, then stuck his finger in his mouth, tasting me. He held the finger to my mouth and I took it, tasting myself.

"You've wanted this for a long time, haven't you?" he asked and unzipped his pants.

I nodded shyly.

"You've wanted me to fuck you," he said. "Now I'm going to. How does that make you feel?"

"It makes me feel good."

"Good?"

I nodded.

He sighed as if this were the answer he wanted all along but was somehow disappointed by it. He took his cock out and forced my mouth to it. I gobbled it up, sucking at him so hard he had to hold me back.

He pushed it in then. And fucked me, grabbing my legs and putting them on his shoulders. This allowed him to go deeper inside me, deeper and deeper and deeper, making me gasp and grunt like an animal. He hammered into me until I screamed with pleasure. I pulled his face to mine and sucked on his tongue, sucked and moaned and began come and come and come! He was coming to. Just before he did, he pushed me back and stuck his cock in my mouth, spewing his hot cum into my mouth. I took it and sucked it dry, then I grabbed him and kissed him, pushing his cum back into his mouth and we shared it. We kissed and kissed until our mouths were sore and we didn't have anything else to give.

"Kristine?" he said, not looking at me.

"Sir?"

"You're fired."

"Damn," I said and bit at his nipple. "And I really needed this gig, too."

He eyed me from the corner of his eye and cracked up. I laughed with him and we laughed until tears formed in our eyes. Then I began to tickle him and he tickled me back until I screamed for him to stop, getting so mad at him that I beat his back with my fist.

"STOP IT! YOU'RE KILLING ME!"

He finally stopped and said, "Come on, let's order a pizza. I'm starving."

The other woman.

It was inevitable. Something was bound to happen. I was snapped out of my sick, happy world one day while I was taking a walk around the Quarter. I'd just stopped at a shop near Jackson Square and was proceeding on to the casino where I was going to meet Jackie to play some nickel slots, then we were going to have a late lunch, then I was going to go home.

Then I saw him.

There he was walking along happily with her, some woman. He assisted her all the way to his car, placing a hand on the small of her back almost as if to make sure she didn't tip over. To anchor her.

Her. Her. Who was she? His secretary? His lover? His sister? He didn't have a sister. *Who was she?* And what was she doing with him? Obviously they'd been out to lunch; it was about two in the afternoon.

I watched as he smiled at her as she whispered something in his ear before getting into the car. He nodded and glanced in my direction. I didn't move. I wanted him to see me. He didn't. I was only a face in the crowd to him, someone anonymous. Unknown.

What struck me as odd was the way he handled himself around her. Gently, reserved. It was puzzling. That's the way he was acting right then. Ambiguous. Not like himself. He rarely smiled. He did smile. Some. When he was pleased.

But with her, he acted well behaved. He used his manners. He held gently to the small of her back, pushing her gently into the car, smiling nicely as she swung her legs in. Smiling as he got in after her.

I was so jealous I couldn't see straight.

The car pulled away almost immediately. I raced towards it on foot and followed it until it disappeared into the traffic.

My first instinct was the leave. Again. I wanted out. When things got tough, I fled. It was my nature to avoid conflict. But why should I leave? And, more importantly, why should I let him get away with it?

It wasn't jealousy I felt. No. That's a lie. It was jealousy. That petty little insecurity that feeds on anger. I was suddenly flushed with anger. As soon as the car disappeared, I was angry. Mad. Fighting mad. My ears roared with it. How could he? How dare he? Those were my smiles she was stealing. They belonged to me!

I hung my head, on the verge of tears. Betrayal set in. I had been betrayed. I kept repeating, *How could he?* over and over and over. I began to walk and I walked a long time, ignoring everyone on the streets, ignoring the Mississippi River to my right. I ignored my date with Jackie, pushed it from my mind and walked for about an hour, then two. I walked until I had blisters on my feet and I walked until I found myself in front of the house, staring at it, my decadent prison. My home. His home. Where we belonged to one another and to no one else.

Should I go in or keep walking? What should I do? Everything in my bones told me to go in, proceed with what was to come. Something else told me to leave, to pack it in, to run away. But I'd been running a long time. Running from one relationship to another, never finding anything worth sticking around for. Was this worth sticking it out? And, if so, why was it so worthy? It was the worst relationship I'd ever been in, yet the best. I played games, I submitted, I relented, I shook with passion inside this relationship. No one had ever given me this. No one ever would, I knew.

I walked in and decided to wait on him.

He called around five that afternoon. He called and set up our latest game. He said he wanted me to pack a picnic lunch, grab a blanket and go to the park.

"Then undress," he said. "Recline backwards. I'll be there at six."

He hung up. I hung up and sat down, put my head in my hands and cried. We'd already played this game. I'd done as he said, found a somewhat secluded area and did exactly as he told me. He fed me the food from the basket and kissed me all over. It was one of the better games. Easy enough to do.

I hated it. I hated that game. It was boring to me. Not much of a challenge. I wasn't going.

I stood and went upstairs, where I crawled into the bed, covered myself and fell asleep.

He woke me up a few hours later. He was angry.

"Where were you?" he demanded to know.

I ignored him and stared at a picture on the wall, concentrating on that picture, tracing the lines of it with my eyes, then back again.

He touched my shoulder. "Where were you?"

"I don't like that game," I said quietly, not taking my eyes from the picture.

"It doesn't matter if you like it or not," he said.

"We all have our limitations."

He pulled me back and forced me to look him in the eye by holding my head still.

"Why didn't you go?"

"I told you," I said. "I don't like that game."

"That's no excuse."

I didn't respond.

"Are you sick?" he asked.

"Yes," I said. "I am very sick."

"What's the matter?" he said, turning on the concern.

"Nothing."

He sighed heavily and shook his head. "Then why are you acting like this?"

"Acting like what?"

"Like something is wrong. You know what I'm talking about."

I glared at him. If he only knew what I knew about him. If he only knew, he'd be sorry then. I would tell him.

"I saw you today," I said.

"Oh?" he asked and his eyebrows shot up.

"Oh, yeah," I said. "I saw you with her."

"Her?"

"The woman who was getting in your car."

He studied me, then turned around. "So?"

"Who is she?"

"She's a client."

"Oh really?"

"Yes."

The sad fact was, I wanted her to be his lover. I wanted something on him. I wanted it so much, I made myself believe it. So I could start to hate him and get out, out, out! I don't know why I wanted out. I'd never been so happy and content in all of my life living with him. But it scared me. It scared the shit right out of me. He had so much control, I wanted some of it back. I wanted to be in control. I knew I'd never be, though. And that I might as well give up. But there was that little something in me that refused to let me relinquish it all to him.

But she wouldn't do. The woman. This woman. Who, really, wasn't anything to him. I knew that. Even if he had fucked her, she didn't mean anything to him. Not like I did. And that scared me even worse, knowing he felt the same way about me as I did about him. It scared me because I was afraid we would both spiral out of control and explode.

"And what type of client is she?" I asked, giving it up, sending the argument to bed.

"You know," he said. "I don't like to discuss business at home."

My face burned along with my ears, neck and shoulders. My entire body just lit up like a Christmas tree. I was shaking now, shaking with fury. *How dare he!?*

I sat up, leaned over and slapped the side of his smug head. He didn't even flinch. He acted as though he expected me to do that, to slap him. I tensed. I thought he was going to do the same. When you're in a volatile relationship, you tend to expect these things. I tensed and waited.

He didn't slap me. He stood, went to the door, opened it, walked through, and then closed it gently.

I was stunned.

Of course, I followed him. I let an hour pass, then I ran down the stairs, calling for him. He didn't answer. I ran through all the rooms searching for him. He was nowhere to be found.

He stayed gone overnight. I fell asleep in his chair in the study. I'd fallen asleep crying, wondering if he was ever going to come back. Wondering what I had done that was so bad. I knew I shouldn't have slapped him, but he *spanked* me and we fought all the time. So what was a little slap?

But of course, when he spanked me, we were usually in the throes of a game.

When he came home, he didn't wake me. He came in and sat in the other chair and watched me until I woke up. He sat there staring at me like I was an object of some kind. Like he was trying to figure out what the hell to do with me.

When I opened my eyes, I didn't smile. He didn't either.

He said quietly, "She's a client of mine. That's all. We were on a business lunch. Take it or leave it."

I took it. And the games began again.

The stranger.

"We're going to meet at a party. Walk in like you don't know anyone. I'll be there around eight. Pretend you don't know me."

"Okay."

"And Kristine?"

"Yes?"

"Wear that little plaid mini-skirt. It really shows off your legs."

I smiled. He loved my legs, their shape, the muscles in my claves. He told me I had diamond calves that people would kill for. Before him, I didn't think my legs were anything special.

"Got it."

"Oh, and one more thing," he said, lowering his voice. "Don't talk to anyone you don't know."

"Frank, I don't know any of those people."

"Exactly."

I rolled my eyes and we hung up.

I arrived at the party around eight. It was just down the street from the house, so I walked by myself. I nervously rang the door and a butler let me in. The host and hostess greeted me, smiling. The host stared at my legs, then caught my eye. I smiled at him. I knew what he was up to.

"I'm Kristine," I told them and held out my hand. "I'm a friend of Frank's."

"Oh!" they exclaimed and shook my hand warmly.

"So you're a friend of Frank's?" the host asked.

I nodded but didn't say another word. The hostess gave me a little smile and, luckily, a couple walked in behind me so their attention was diverted and I was able to walk away from them quickly, going into the living room. I noticed all the people in there were very elegantly dressed. I looked around for Frank, but didn't see him. A few people smiled at me and a few nodded, but other than that, I didn't really communicate with anyone. No one seemed to know who I was and that made me feel very vulnerable. I was almost afraid I'd get kicked out.

Nine o'clock came and went and Frank still didn't show. I was trying to have a conversation with a man who had this awful looking toupee on his head. I couldn't concentrate on him and all his words come out in a jumble: Egg salad…business associate…the color green…olives…

I smiled at him and forced my eyes away from his toupee. He didn't force his eyes away from my tits or ass. I allowed him a look; I didn't mind it at all.

I felt a hand on my shoulder. I turned to see Frank. I smiled at him.

"Yes?"

"Do I know you?" he asked.

I smiled at him like I was considering. The toupee guy had asked me the very same thing.

"Uh, no. I don't think so."

He grinned and turned to lean against the couch we were standing behind. I smiled back and raised one eyebrow.

"Hey, Frank," the man said.

"Hello," he said without taking his eyes off me.

I tensed. What was he going to do?

Frank pointed a finger at me. "I know who you are. You're the debutante from Alabama."

I almost cracked up. I didn't. I concealed my laughter and said, "Oh, you found me out."

He nodded. "What's it like being a debutante?"

"Boring as hell."

He laughed softly and the other man stared at him, then back at me.

The man asked, "You're from the Williams family, right?"

I nodded, going with it. "Yes."

"I know your father very well!"

"Really?" I asked just as Frank jerked his head. I stared at him and he held his finger upside down and rotated it. I obeyed, turned and took one step back towards him.

"Yes," the man continued. "I did business with him a while back."

"That's good to hear," I said and felt Frank's hand on the back of my shirt.

"He's a great man, your father."

"Really? That's funny because he's always been a bastard to me," I said and tensed. Frank's finger slid down my back, between my ass cheeks and was now lifting the bottom of my skirt up.

The man eyed him, but continued. "Uh, what was that?"

"Nothing," I said as I felt Frank's finger slide along the seam of my g-string.

"So, what do you do?" he asked, still eyeing Frank.

"I'm a stripper," I said, just to see if he was paying attention.

He wasn't. He was watching Frank and what he was doing to me. I could tell he was getting off on it, which was fine by me. I smiled at him, but he didn't notice.

He said, "Oh, that's an interesting field."

"Yes, it is," I said and felt his finger on my clit, arousing it. I almost stopped him, but I couldn't. His finger went up into my pussy and moved around a bit, while his other one stayed on my clit. I moved my hips just a little and felt the full force of finger. Just as he was about to make me come, he pulled his finger out and staring at the man, he stuck it in his mouth and sucked it dry. The man, having just taken a sip of scotch, nearly choked.

Frank touched my shoulder and gave me one tiny kiss on the back of my neck.

"Well, it was nice talking to you, Miss Williams," he said and walked away.

"You, too," I called as if we we'd just had a pleasant conversation.

The man smiled and leaned in towards me. "So, how about if we go find somewhere to sit and talk?"

I turned on my heel. "Thanks anyway, but I have to get home."

I hurried out of the house, slipped my heels off and started to run, hoping to beat Frank to the house.

"Kristine!"

I turned and saw him standing by a Rolls Royce. He jerked his head towards it. I grinned and flew over to him and we got in the back. I fell down on my back and he was on top of me immediately. I wrapped my legs around his waist as he tore off my g-sting and pushed his hard cock into me. I gasped and grabbed his head, kissing him passionately, grinding myself against him as he squeezed my tit with the palm of his hand. It didn't take much at all. The orgasm—for both of us—was instantaneous. We were that turned on.

We laid there gasping for a moment then I looked around the soft blue interior of the car.

"Kristine," he said.

"Yes?"

"I thought I told you not to talk to strangers."

I smiled and hugged his neck. "Frank, give it a rest."

He chuckled and nuzzled my neck. "Okay."

"Whose car is this?"

"I have no idea."

Silly games.

As I said, they were silly games. We loved them. We loved every part of them. Each day brought a new game, a different game, a game that was better than the one before. A game that always ended in us fucking like animals.

I didn't take them seriously, but I was seriously falling in love with him. I couldn't help myself. I would wait all day for his call. I stopped seeing my friends. I didn't want any friends. I didn't want anyone but him.

The next game changed my mind about him. It hurt me. Somehow, I was convinced I loved him. Maybe it really wasn't love, but infatuation, obsession that had been realized and had spiraled out of control.

"There's an alley beside the Hotel Brazil," he said.

"An alley?"

"Yes, an alley," he said. "Meet me there."

"In the alley?" I asked.

"Yeah," he said and his voice took on a tone of excitement. "I thought…Never mind. Just show up. You know what to wear."

Short skirt. Tight top. High heels. My typical uniform.

"Okay," I said.

"I'll see you then."

"Okay. Oh, by the way, what am I today?" I asked and glanced at the clock.

"You're a whore."

He hung up.

I was slightly stunned. A whore? I was whore? For some reason, that didn't sit well with me. I certainly didn't think of myself as a whore. Or maybe I felt like a whore, living with him, off of him, all he ever got in return was the unlimited use of my body.

Ah, hell, it was only a game.

I convinced myself of that and rushed around getting ready, then took a cab to the hotel and found the alley, which was very narrow and, thankfully, deserted. I sniffed. God, it stank. So rank. Garbage was overflowing in the dumpster.

Did whores come here to fuck their johns? I didn't know. If I was a whore, they'd have to pay for a room. I'm sorry, but I wasn't into fucking in alleys.

I waited for a little while, swinging my pocketbook, then laughed out loud, thinking about Frank. This must be one of his older fantasies, meeting a whore in an alley and fucking her, then…What would he do after? Would he pay me? And how much? What was someone like me worth? A grand? At least. Fuck that. Five grand, especially if they didn't pay for a room.

I stared up at the sky. It was darkening. He'd better hurry up. The afternoon lull was almost over and soon this very alley would probably be crawling with the real hookers.

I heard footsteps. They were his, I could tell. Heavy, deliberate footsteps, always walking quickly and with a purpose. I glanced up and smiled. He was walking towards me with a very determined look.

"Hey, baby," I said. "How's about a date?"

He nodded, eying me. "How much?"

"For you," I said and traced a line along the collar of his shirt. "Free."

"No," he said, shaking his head. "I can pay. I want to pay."

"How much you got?"

"Whatever it takes."

I eyed him as if I were considering. "Umm…I'll give you a discount. A couple hundred."

He nodded. "Deal."

"Cool," I said and smiled at him.

"What's your name?"

I considered. "Ummm…Gabrielle."

"I'm Ted."

"Nice to meet you, Ted. Are you ready to fuck?"

He nodded. I set my pocketbook on the ground and before I could stand back up, he came at me and began to tug at my skirt. I pushed him off.

"Hey," I said. "Why don't we get a room?"

"I don't have the time," he said hurriedly. "I've been thinking about this all day."

"Thinking about what?"

"Fucking a whore."

Again, that unsettling feeling sank into me. I almost pushed him away and walked off, but it was only a game. Right?

"Okay," I said. "Let's do it."

I grabbed for his face to kiss him, but he pushed me away and shoved me up against the course brick wall. What the hell? I pushed him back, but he pushed me back again, grabbing my crotch, pulling my skirt up, and sticking his stiff cock in me without a word. He fucked me dry, not caring if I was wet or ready or even enjoying it.

I was almost in shock. What the hell was he doing? He fucked me for a good five minutes and anytime I tried to kiss him, he wouldn't let me. He only sucked on my tits and fucked me.

"Frank—"

"Shut up," he muttered.

What the hell was wrong with him?

He finished and pulled away from me, then zipped his pants, took out his wallet and threw a couple hundred dollars at me. I didn't grab for the bills and they fell to the ground. I was stunned. What the hell was this all about?

"How does it feel to be a whore?" he asked.

"What?" I asked, aghast.

"You're a whore, aren't you?"

I moved away from the wall. "Frank—"

He pushed me back and whispered in my ear, "You're a whore today and I want to know how it feels. How do you like being a whore?"

That flew all over me, I was all of a sudden angry. I hated him with every fiber in my being. Maybe it upset me because maybe, just maybe, that's what he thought of me. Nothing more than a body, something to stick his cock in. A whore.

I shoved him off.

"I'll show you what kind of whore I am," I hissed back and kneed his balls. He doubled over in pain and moaned. I whacked him upside the head, stood, pulled my skirt down, grabbed my pocket-book and ran out of the alley.

"You can't leave! Our time isn't up!"

"Oh, it is, it is certainly up, asshole!"

Fuck him! I ran as fast as I could before he could get to me. I was so angry, I saw red. I ran to the closest bar, stopped, caught my breath and went in.

I'd show him. If he wanted me to be a whore, I'd be whore. I'd be the best fucking whore in the world.

I surveyed the room and picked out my target. There he was. A young man. Early twenties. Big feet. Cute. Easy target. Good enough. I sashayed over to him, sat in the seat next to him and smiled. He straightened up and grinned from ear to ear like he couldn't believe his luck.

"Hi," he said.

I didn't beat around the bush. I said, "Hundred bucks."

"Excuse me."

"I'll fuck you for a hundred bucks."

"Really?" He leaned back and checked me out, as if to see if I was serious. "Really?"

I nodded. "Give it to me."

He stared at me like he didn't believe me.

"I'm serious," I said. "Get it out."

He pulled his wallet out and fumbled with it, counting money. "I only got fifty."

I held out my hand. "Give it to me. I'll give you a discount."

He handed it to me. I shoved it in my bra, pulled him up and started out the door.

"Where are we going?" he asked.

"In the alley," I said and he followed me to the same place Frank had just fucked me.

"Here?" he asked, looking uncertain about the whole thing now.

"Shh," I said and kissed him. His lips were chapped and he had that after cigarette taste in his mouth. I tried not to think about that as I allowed him to kiss me back. He kissed like a teenager. It was all tongue. I felt his crotch. He was hard. He'd do.

I unzipped his pants, pulled my skirt up and helped him put it in. He fucked me. I stood there and let him, not feeling any of it, just like a whore. I felt tears stream down my face. I felt so bad, so awful. I wanted him off me. But I was whore and whores don't do that. They let their customers finish. I decided to fuck him back, to give him his money's worth. He deserved it. He didn't deserve some whore who didn't like her job.

He moaned and buried his head in my neck as I held onto him. I felt him move faster and knew he was about to come. I was relieved. I was so relieved. I was leaving. I was leaving. I was leaving! I made the decision as he fucked me. I would go home. I might go to Florida. Start a new life. But I was leaving. I was leaving Frank. He'd never see me again. All my stuff was in his house. But I had fifty bucks. No car. My car was at his house. I could get a bus ticket to somewhere.

I started to cry harder, knowing it was going to be hard as hell to leave, but knowing I should. Why did he have to do that? Why? I didn't like that game. I hated being called a whore. Guys in the strip-club would call us whores when we wouldn't fuck them. "So what?" they'd say. "You take it off. What's the difference?"

Was there a difference? Was there? What fine line was there, separating me from the others, from the whores? Maybe there wasn't a difference. Maybe all men classified all women as whores, like we sometimes classified all of them as jerks.

Maybe Frank classified me as a whore.

And that's what had done it. That's why I had freaked out. Why I wanted to leave, to run away. Did he think I was a whore simply doing his bidding? Doing everything he wanted and asking for more?

Yeah. He must feel like that.

Suddenly, the guy was pulled off me and thrown on the ground. I gasped and looked Frank right in the eye. I scowled. He looked at the guy, who looked up at him in disbelief.

"What is your problem, buddy?" the guy asked.

Frank pulled him up and punched him in the nose.

"Hey!" he yelled, holding his nose. "What'd you that for?"

He gave him another punch.

"She's a whore, man," he groaned.

"Yeah, she's a whore, but she's my whore, motherfucker!"

This time he went at him, pummeling him with his fists. Beating him to a bloody pulp. I watched in horror. I had to go. Go. Go now.

I turned and raced out of the alley. Frank was immediately on my heels, pulling me off the crowed street and into his limo. He shoved me in, got in, slammed the door and the car took off.

"Why did you do that?" I asked.

He was breathing hard, but he was trying to stay calm. "How could *you* do that?"

"I did what you told me to do!" I screamed in his face. "I'm a whore, remember?!"

He backhanded me. I fell against the seat and groaned as my head swam. He'd never done that before, backhand me, like a pimp back-hands his whores. I held my face and stared at him, feeling all the love I had for him drain from my body. I couldn't give it to him. I didn't want to give it to him. Not anymore.

I took it back. All the love I had for him, I took back. And I was leaving him, no matter what, I was leaving. He was no better than any other man I'd ever had. Fuck him anyway.

I grabbed the door handle and tried to get out. It was locked. From the driver's side. I couldn't get out. I banged on the window.

"Let me out, Tony!"

Tony ignored me.

"Fucker!" I yelled at him.

"Shut up," Frank said.

"Fuck you!" I screamed and pulled on the door. "Let me out! I'm leaving!"

"Leaving?" he said and grabbed my arm, pulling me next to him. "And go where? To your little shitty town? To where? You got nowhere to go but home. With me."

"I would rather die than go home with you!" I spat in his face. "Now let me out!"

He released me and turned to stare out the window. I almost pan-icked. But I had to stay calm. Once we got to the house, I'd jump out first, then run like hell to get away.

And I would not, I repeat, would not, look back.

The wine cellar.

Before I had a chance to put my plan into action, he opened his door, grabbed my arm and pulled me across the seat and out of the car, then into the house. I beat at him with my free arm and screamed bloody murder. Which he did not heed. Neither did the neighbors.

He pulled me through the house, down to the basement and to the wine cellar. He shoved me on the floor, left the room, and locked the door behind him. I stared up at the ceiling. Only one bulb hung from it.

Oh shit. Shit. *SHIIIIIITTTT!*

I jumped up and ran to the door, beating it with my hands and screaming. I couldn't get out of here. The only way out was that door and it was old, made of rough wood and at least three inches thick. It made my hands bleed as I beat it. But I didn't care. Someone had to hear me. Pierre, the cook. Maybe even Tony would take pity and rescue me.

I beat that door for ten minutes. Then I beat it for an hour, three. And no one came. I was a prisoner. I wasn't getting out.

I was all alone.

Just for fun, I broke a few of the old wine bottles, laughing crazily to myself, thinking about how mad it would make him when he found out. Then I thought I might need them. So I decided to make a party of the whole thing and get drunk.

I looked around. No corkscrew. Huh. I grabbed a bottle, slammed the neck against the shelf and cracked it open. I took a drink and spit it out. Good. No glass slivers. It had been a clean break.

I drank the whole thing and got another bottle from a very good year. I sat down and drank the bottle clean, threw it the side and started to cry. I cried for a long damn time. I cried until my eyes were dry.

I begged the ceiling, "Please, God, let me out of here. Make him stop this."

Then I had to pee. Real bad. I looked around. Of course, there wasn't a bathroom in here. Fuck it. I walked over to a corner, squatted and did my business. Let him worry about it. I didn't care.

I finally fell asleep. I slept for a long time on that cold, concrete floor. When I awoke, there was a tray of food by the door. If that's what you could call it. Bread and water. Pate. Pate! He knew I hated pate! The bastard. Served on a silver platter. I was definitely a prisoner.

But I was hungry. I gobbled the food and water up and threw the tray at the door.

No one came.

I wandered around in circles for a while then I sat down and cried. I schemed. When he came to let me out, I'd hit him with a wine bottle. Get him real good. Make him bleed.

When he came...

When would that be? How long had I been here? I looked up at the light. It flickered. Oh fuck. No. *Nooo!* It flickered again and went out. And I was in the dark.

I hated him then. More than ever, I hated him. I really, really did. But what could I do? I was stuck. I knew he had purposely thrown me in the cellar so he wouldn't be tempted to beat me. Like he had the first time I'd really pissed him off.

What a great guy.

I'd never give him anything anymore. He had ruined it all. By acting like an animal, by treating me like a whore, he had ruined it.

But why should I go? Where should I go?

I decided I'd stay. I'd play his games and I'd steal from him. I'd be that whore he wanted me to be. I'd grub for money. I'd ask for it. And when I was ready to leave, I'd leave a rich woman.

He deserved no better. He couldn't love me. He didn't love me. If he loved me, he would have never, ever treated me like that. I didn't like being treated like a whore. That was my pet peeve. It got under my skin so bad it drove me crazy. I hated, and I mean hated, men who treated women like shit. Like whores.

I would be nice. I'd play his games. Hell, I'd even enjoy them, but something in me, God knows what it was, would not allow me to give him my love. Not anymore. He'd almost had me. He wasn't going to get me anymore. He could fuck me, but that would be all. He could not have me.

I would be his whore. Nothing more, nothing less.

                  🍁   🍁   🍁

He called softly, "Are you ready to come out?"

I sat up and rubbed my eyes. The light was back on. He'd replaced the bulb.

"Frank?"

"No," he said. "It's Tony."

"Tony?"

I was almost disappointed.

"Yeah, it's me," he said softly. "Are you ready to come out?"

"Where's Frank?"

"I dunno. But I can't let you stay down here much longer."

I focused on him. He was a good man. Why couldn't I have picked a guy like him? He was big, kind. Yeah, we know what was wrong with him. He was boring. He wouldn't put me in wine cellars or beat the living hell out of me.

"How long have I been here?"

"It's been a couple of days."

A couple of days? Surely not. I had slept most of those days, though. Time moves quick when you sleep all the time. Like when you get sick and all you can do is sleep. You get sick on Monday and the next thing you know, it's Thursday.

"Kristine?"

I stared at him. "Does Frank know you're letting me out?"

He shook his head sadly.

I curled back up in a ball and closed my eyes.

"You've got to leave now," he said. "He'll be back anytime."

"No, Tony," I said. "But thank you anyway."

"Kristine, you're crazy!" he muttered.

"I know, but I can't let you do this for me. Please go."

He sighed but didn't argue. He shut the door quietly and I fell back to sleep.

When I awoke, Frank was curled up next to me, a blanket covering us. I was relieved to see him. I put my arms around him, he kissed my hand and put it next to his cheek. I closed my eyes and we slept. I had been in there two whole days.

We never mentioned the incident again.

🍁   🍁   🍁

Even though Frank could be a complete bastard, he took good care of me. When we woke up, he led me to the kitchen, letting me lean on him as I faked being weak. He prepared me a big breakfast of bacon, eggs and biscuits and gravy. He poured me a coke with ice, just the way I liked it. I made my hand shake as I lifted the fork to my mouth, like I was weak from being "starved". He stared at my hand

and shame came over his face. Good. Good enough for him. I wanted him to feel bad for what he'd done. He deserved no better.

He took the fork out of my hand and fed me, like I was a baby. He wiped the corners of my mouth off, held the straw to my lips so I could drink the coke, and kissed my cheek.

He told me he loved me. Loved me. Loved me, loved me, loved me.

I smiled, repeated his line to him and ate.

When breakfast was over, he took me upstairs, where he drew me a bath. He put me in the tub and washed me from head to toe, again, like I was a child. He did so gently, patiently.

Then he combed my hair, towel dried my body and took me to bed, where he laid me down and began to kiss my body, every inch of it. Soft, whisper kisses. Kisses that made me moan and pull him on top of me. Again, we made love. We didn't fuck as we did before. When it was over, I fell asleep in his arms, as content as a…As a baby.

Blindfolded.

"Here," he said, slipping a white silk scarf around my eyes. "Put it on."

I smiled and tensed. It had taken him awhile to warm up to the idea of blindfolding me. But I knew it was coming. He'd hint at it every so often, and I'd smile and say, "Whatever you like. You're in control."

Whatever you like. You're in control. And not me.

"Lay back."

I scooted back on the bed and tried to relax. I felt his fingertips glide along my body, stopping every so often to tease me. I reached out for him. He pushed my hand back down.

"No," he said and I heard him rise and move away from me.

"Where are you going?" I asked.

"Shh…"

I laid there quietly for a few moments, tensed and ready. I could feel him bend down in front of me. I wanted to reach out and touch him, but I couldn't see anything. Which was the point of it all. I didn't really like the blindfold because of that reason. I liked to have all my senses alert and ready. Just in case.

"Are you ready for me?" he asked softly.

I sighed. He took that as a "yes".

"Relax."

I attempted to relax, then I felt a light, tickling sensation.

"Can you feel that?"

"Oh, yes."

The sensation had started on my knee and was slowly moving up my body, cruising by my inner thigh, trailing along the outer lips of my pussy, skirting up my belly, between my breasts, then stopping to caress each nipple, then it lingered on my face.

"Ahh..."

He gave a slight sigh as if my response pleased him. The sensation was now in the crook of my arm. What was it? A feather?

"Ummm..." I moaned. "What is it?"

"A mink stole."

Oh. Mink. It was so soft. Light. It tickled me just to the point of pleasure and never went beyond. It slid along my body, readying it for more. And there was more on the way, I could tell.

"See if you can tell me what this is," he said.

I waited. Then I felt something cool, almost cold, slide down between my breasts, then puddle onto my stomach. It bubbled slightly.

I smiled. "Champagne."

I could tell he nodded. He bent over and began to lick the champagne off my body, slurping it up into his mouth then he leaned over and pressed his lips against mine. I opened my mouth and he deposited the champagne. I swallowed.

"Thank you," I said and smiled.

"Tell me," he said. "Do you like being blindfolded?"

I considered. What's not to like? Especially since it had all been good. Maybe it'd get better?

"Yes," I said.

"Good," came his reply.

I heard the clink of ice cubes in a glass, then I felt an ice cube between my legs, inside my pussy and it was slowly melting, making me numb down there. His face was down there, his tongue gently probing it in, puckering his lips until it disappeared.

Ahh, that felt good.

Two fingers were in me then, twisting, finding my spot. My hips rose off the bed. He pushed them back down.

"No."

"What?" I moaned and tried to raise my hips to meet his lips again. But he had moved. I put my hand between my legs and started to rub, but he took it off.

"No. Not yet."

"*PLEASE!*"

"No. Not yet."

I grunted and groaned and shook, but he wouldn't let me. He wouldn't let me touch myself to bring myself any sort of release. And it was killing me. I was so wound up, so turned on, so hot I could have spontaneously combusted.

"You're not very good at this game," he said.

"Why?"

"You want to touch yourself too soon."

"What's wrong with that?"

"Nothing, if all you're concerned with is getting off."

I sighed, my shoulders slumping. He was right, but I had somehow thought that was the point. Of sex, I mean. To get off.

"You see," he said and I could tell he was looking over at me. "The point is arousal, so much arousal that is never fulfilled by orgasm at once. You build it up. So, when you have your orgasm, it's more intense than it could ever be before."

Had he read that in a book?

"How would you know?" I asked.

He sighed. "It builds up for both of us, Kristine."

"And how would you know?"

He snapped, "It's just an idea I had!"

He jerked the scarf off my face. I blinked in the bright light. He glared at me. I looked away.

"Do you want that, Kristine? Do you want that intensity?"

"Yeah, of course I do," I said, wondering exactly what it entailed. Wondering exactly what would be expected of me.

"Can you handle it?" he asked softly.

I stared him dead in the eye and responded, "Of course I could handle it."

He nodded slowly, not very pleased with my answer. "No, you couldn't handle it."

"Yes, I can!"

"Then do this," he said. "Refrain from touching yourself. All day tomorrow. And after I've gone to sleep."

"I don't do it that much!"

"No, you don't have to because we fuck every day. Today we're not going to fuck. Or tomorrow. Got it?"

I sighed. Well, I could always lie to him.

"Kristine?"

"Okay. I'll do it."

You will be punished. Severely.

I sat on edge all day, waiting for his call. It didn't come. He didn't come home until late and when he did, he ignored me, went up the stairs and into the bedroom. Without a single word.

I willed myself not to succumb to any anger. I willed myself up the stairs and into the bedroom.

He was in the bathroom, brushing his teeth. I went in, sat on the commode and stared straight ahead.

He ignored me.

"Frank?"

He didn't respond.

"Why are you mad at me?"

"You know why."

"I do?"

He shook his head. "Yes, you do. Now leave me alone."

He was right. Damn him. I had to give it all over to him to experience this intensity he wanted us to experience. I knew that. But I wasn't ready. I didn't know if I would ever be ready for it.

"Did you masturbate today?" he asked.

I jerked at his question then stared back at the wall, almost embarrassed. Well, yeah, I had.

"No, I didn't," I lied.

He stared back at me, his head nodding slightly. "Bring me your toys."

"What?"

"You heard me."

"No," I said, crossing my arms, thinking of my vibrator. No way was I giving that up.

He sighed and went back to looking at himself in the mirror. He ran his hand over his face once. I sighed.

He said, "You masturbated today, didn't you?"

It wasn't so much a question as an accusation.

"Yeah, you did."

How in the hell did he know that? It's like he could just tell, even after I'd lied to him. He must be psychic or something.

"How do you know this?" I asked.

"I can see it in your eyes," he said, all knowing. "I can see that you did it when I asked you not to."

I almost cried. I wasn't going to. I had tried not to masturbate, but then I started having this fantasy of us and the next thing I knew, I was on the bed giving it to myself, coming and coming quick. After it was over, I had another. And another, until I was exhausted.

"How do you know?" I asked.

"I just do," he said. "I know you. You never listen to anything but your cunt."

I sighed. He was right. But why did that make him so mad? I decided to make it up to him. I went behind him and slid my hands up his back. He stiffened. But he didn't move.

I tiptoed and kissed the back of his neck, pushing my hands into his hair. Suddenly, he whirled around, grabbed my wrists and twisted me until I was nose to nose with him.

"I am not in the mood," he said, then moved away from me.

Tears sprang up in my eyes. I hated him then. I hated every cell in his body. I hated his blue eyes. His handsome face, his cologne.

I peered around the doorway and watched as he got into bed. I loved him. I loved every part of him, even this. No, no. Not loved. Wanted. I wanted every part of him. There was a difference. It was all lust now, the love wasn't there anymore. But it didn't make me want him any less. I knew he was holding out on me. Making me wait. Making me want it. Making me want it so bad I'd explode.

I went to the bed and sat down, not looking at him.

He eyed me and sighed as he said, "It's just that I want you to give more of yourself."

I was stunned slightly. *More* of myself? More of *me*? I was giving him everything I knew how to give and more than I'd ever given anyone else. I'd taken shit from him I would have never taken from any other man. I put up with it because I'd never felt this way about anyone else. He knew it. I knew it. It was no secret. I would pretend to love him, give to him until I was ready to leave. Then I'd turn it off. That was the plan.

"What are you talking about?" I asked.

"You hold back."

"I do not!" I said, indignantly.

"Yes," he said. "Yes, you do."

"How?"

"You always want that quick orgasm, instead of holding out for more. You're like a teenage boy."

My face flushed. Maybe he was right, to a certain extent, but wasn't that what sex was all about in the first place? Getting off? I wasn't into Tantric or any of that *Kama Sutra* stuff. I liked fucking and fucking liked me and we went well together. Why mess with a good thing?

"I don't know what you're talking about," I said and crossed my arms.

He pointed at my arms. "That's what I'm talking about."

I rolled my eyes.

"Yeah, go ahead and roll your eyes. You're very good at that, aren't you?"

"Fuck off," I said and started to rise.

He pushed me back down on the bed. I struggled against him for a moment, then he kissed me and I melted. Oh, yeah. Oh, baby. I opened my mouth just as he pulled away and he pulled quickly, abruptly, as if I disgusted him. As soon as I melted, he pulled away. And refused to let me pull him back down.

"That's what I'm talking about."

"What?!" I half-yelled, getting pissed off.

"Our games, these games, are fine," he said. "For beginners. We're not beginners anymore, are we?"

I studied him. I tried to figure him out, I really did. I couldn't. I just wasn't getting it.

He leaned and whispered in my ear, "I want to show you something. Stay here."

He jumped up and ran into the closet. I sat on the bed and wondered what the hell he was doing. I could hear him rummaging around in the closet. He came back a moment later carrying something, holding something behind his back, like it was a surprise. I eyed his arm, wondering what his hand held. Candy? A rose? Sometimes he brought me little gifts like that. Once I got a Cartier watch. Once a pair of diamond earrings. What was it this time? When he finally pulled it out, my jaw dropped to the floor.

He had a switch. Not a rose. Not candy. And certainly not a watch. It was a switch, the kind pulled from a tree to swat the backs of children's legs when they're being brats. The kind my mother used on me from time to time to keep me in line.

A switch.

He cracked it in front of me. I almost cracked up.

"May I?" he asked.

Before I could think of an answer, the switch came down and hit me smack dab on my outer thigh. I screamed with pain as it cut right through my skin and scorched the muscle. It hurt like hell. Like a papercut. That's what it felt like. Tears sprang up in my eyes, burning into them.

He bent down in front of me and whispered, barely audible, "Did you like how that felt?"

I began to shake my head. No. That would be a negative. It hurt too bad.

"Kristine," he said. "Tell me. Tell me now. Did you like how that felt?"

No. I didn't. I couldn't. How could I like that? He was inflicting pain on me. I didn't like that. I didn't like pain.

"Tell me. Please?"

I didn't like it. I didn't like it. I didn't like it.

"Tell me."

What kind of sick person likes something like that?

"Tell me?"

If I liked it, then that would mean…What would that mean?

"Tell me."

Would it mean I was a sick person? That I had been brought to this level by him? What *did* it mean?

"Tell me."

No. No. NO NO NO NO NO!

"Remember the first time I beat you?"

Oh, yeah. How could I forget? I still had scars. Not from the belt, but from the fall, but scars nonetheless. Scars that reminded me of the incident, of his anger towards me. Of my fear.

"Remember how it hurt?"

Of course I remember!

"Remember afterwards? Remember how I took care of you? Remember how it felt, especially afterwards."

I didn't like it. I didn't—

"You liked it, Kristine," he said. "I could tell you liked it. You liked having me in control of you, you being out of control, you liked it. A lot. Didn't you?"

No, I did not.

"You liked it so much you tested me," he said, his face in my hair, near my neck. I could feel his hot, sweet breath. He smelled like mint toothpaste. He smelled so good, fresh, clean. I wanted him so much.

"You've tried to get me that upset again. But it scared the shit out of me. I was scared of it because I was afraid I'd lose control and really hurt you. But now I understand and I'm asking you. Did you like it? Did you like the way it felt to have no control? To not know how it was going to turn out? To give yourself over to that moment?"

That moment. Oh, God, that moment. That moment where nothing made sense and everything else did. That moment where I was at my weakest, yet I'd never felt stronger. That moment where everything fell from the Earth and I could care less. That moment when clarity took over and suddenly I knew what it was all about, all of it. And everything was about that moment. Every single thing. And I'd wanted it back. So I could feel alive, so I could get that close to him again, that under his skin, that close. So close I couldn't breathe if he didn't tell me to.

I knew what he was talking about. And it scared the shit right out of me. I couldn't think. I couldn't think straight. I began to quiver, panic.

"The way you responded to me blew me away. And you've been testing me ever since, trying to make me do it again."

He was lying.

"You've been testing me ever since."

He was telling the truth.

"You accused me of sleeping with another woman so I would hit you. Didn't you?"

The other woman. Oh. Uh…Oh, no. Oh, no. It wasn't about that. It was about me leaving him, finding an escape route so I could take off. That's what it had been about. But even as I sat there and tried to make myself believe it—and it was true to a certain extent—I knew. I knew he was right. He knew me too well. I could never admit it, though. I could never admit wanting to give myself over like that. That would make me as bad as the men who played these games, who inflicted the pain.

"Kristy," my mother would say. "Never trust a man because as soon as you do, they'll be gone. Out the damn door. Just like your damn daddy. And you'll be on your ass. Never, I repeat, never trust one enough to let them have control."

Never, never, never. Never let anyone have any control, have anything on you. They'll use you. They'll treat you like shit. You—

He said, "You liked me taking control and you liked me taking care of you afterwards."

Did I? If he said it and thought it and believed it to be true, than did I as well? Did I believe that?

"You have to know," he whispered, so softly. "You can trust me. Trust me, Kristine. Let's see how far we can go. I would never do anything to you that you couldn't handle."

I wanted to cry, throw up. This was too much, too, too much. I wanted to run away and forget it all. But I couldn't. I was cemented to him now. We both knew we'd already crossed that line and now we were dancing along it, twirling, nearly falling, regaining control and laughing about it.

"Trust me."

Trust. Trust, trust. Trust him.

"Just this once."

This once...Now. Today. This moment. Trust him now. Do it before it's too late. If I didn't accept, it would be over. And I didn't want it to be over. Not yet. I was still having too much fun for that. And I still hadn't robbed him blind like I'd intended after he had thrown me into the wine cellar. I hadn't done it yet because...

I didn't know why.

Then he did it. He gained my trust. He said the one thing he needed to say to win me over.

He said, "We'll take it slow, at first."

I couldn't control myself. I wanted to jump on him, fuck him, and have him fuck me. I wanted to succumb to his every wish, to his every desire. To whatever he wanted.

I breathed, "I'll do it. Just this once."

He smiled. "Then let's do it."

I reached over and found the scarf, which was lying on the night-stand, and handed it to him as an offering. He eyed me.

"Are we going to do it right this time?"

I nodded feebly.

"I don't have much patience," he said. "If you're not committed to this, I will be very angry."

I nodded.

"You sure?"

"Yes."

He said, "Now you have to let me have control. You know that. If you do anything that pisses me off, you will be punished. Severely."

I stiffened. Did he just say that? *You will be punished. Severely.* What exactly did he mean by that? And what did "severely" entail?

I started, "Frank, what—"

"This is your first and your last warning," he said. "You either let me do it or we stop."

Let him do it. Stop. Let him do it. Stop. Surrender or stop. Stop or surrender? Which one?

"Okay," I muttered.

"You have to totally submit to me, Kristine, in order for this to work."

Totally submit. Submit. Submission. Let go. Acquiesce.

I took a deep breath and nodded, staring up at him.

"So are we set here?" he asked, in a very business-like tone.

"We're set."

"Good. I assume you're ready?"

"I'm ready."

He blindfolded me before pushing me back on the bed where he began to undress me. He took his time, loving having me under his control.

"Relax," he whispered.

My senses became alert, ready. Steady. I could hear everything that went on inside the room. His bare feet padding on the wood floor. The ticking of his alarm clock. The vent pushing warm air into the room from above. The soft bed covers. The silk of the comforter.

He rolled me over onto my stomach.

I felt the tip of the switch tracing along my skin. Ever so gentle. It rode along me, forcing me to tremble with anticipation. Then, all of a sudden, it came down and came down hard. Right across my back. *Ouch!* It was the papercut feeling. I hated that.

His lips were on the mark now, kissing it, his hands caressing it, fondling it, easing the pain away. Ah, that was better.

"Would you like another?"

I was so excited, I could barely breathe.

"Yes."

And the switch came down. This time across the back of my thighs. It almost tickled. Then the sensation eased. I felt relief, release. Surrender.

"Can you handle another?"

"No," I said sitting up. "Not just yet."

He got up, turned me over, bent and kissed the tip of my nose. I began to quiver.

"Lie back."

I laid back.

"No touching yourself."

"No touching."

"Promise?"

"Yes," I breathed. "I promise."

His hands were then all over me, the palms sliding along my body, kneading me, bringing all of my senses out. My nipples hardened and wanted his lips. I moved to the side, towards his face, but he pushed me back down.

"I'm warning you."

"About what?" I moaned, teasing him.

"I told you."

"Told me what?" I asked and almost laughed at his seriousness.

All of a sudden, I was turned, flipped onto my stomach and I heard a crack and his belt—not the switch—came down across my ass. I let out a wail that shook the chandelier.

"Why did you do that?" I cried and felt the welt on my ass.

"You know why."

I stiffened and started to take the blindfold off.

"If you take it off," he said methodically. "We won't start this game again."

My hands dropped involuntarily. I couldn't take another day without sex. Even if that meant he was going to give me a few more lashes.

He turned me back over and his hands began to play along my body once more. I moaned. It was killing me to lie there and not do anything. I wanted his hands on me, but more importantly, I wanted my hands on him. I wanted to touch him, his skin. I wanted to pull him tight and hang on forever.

He opened my legs and got between them, positioning himself there. I could tell he was staring at me, at my cunt. This made my juices flow even more, to have him stare at me like that. I moved a little, trying to entice his lips to move in that direction, down there.

"Do you need another lash?" he said as I moved again.

I halted myself. "No."

"Good."

I balled my fists up and waited for him to continue.

His fingers began to play with me then, one went into my pussy, moved around a bit, then the other stroked my ass. The pleasure was so intense, I nearly cried out. I bit my fist and tried to contain the cry. Something came out anyway. I think it was, "Please."

He sighed, got up, turned me over and gave me another lash. This time, it didn't hurt. Well, it did. But it was different. It was so different, like nothing I'd ever felt before. As the belt hit me, I felt a deep surge of power from it, as if it were giving me power. I shivered and began to shake. It took everything in my body to keep me from asking for another.

Then, as soon as it hit, it was gone and I felt light, almost airy.

He turned me back over.

This time, he dove in, eating at me, licking, almost chewing. I moaned. He kept at it. I was almost there, the orgasm was coming and it was coming hard and then…

He stopped. "You're doing it again."

The switch came out and he began to tap me with it, lightly at first, then with more intensity. Tap, tap, tap. It went all over my body, every square inch of my body became alive as the switch played with me, teased me, controlled me. It wasn't painful, not really, it was more of a tickling sensation, just this side of irritating. I laid there and allowed it, allowed it until I couldn't handle it anymore and I screamed for him to stop, but he didn't. I begged and pleaded and I promised myself I wouldn't want it again, that I couldn't take it. It was too much. No orgasm was worth this. But just before I broke, he turned me around and kissed me, sending me into a totally different realm.

"Get up on all fours."

Uh, what? No. You get back down there and finish what you started.

"Now."

I got up on all fours.

He pulled my legs apart and then he began to eat me from behind this time, licking every crevice. I was so wet his face just slid along. He sucked at my clit for a moment, then pulled back and fingered it gently. I moaned and before I knew what I was doing, my hand was on it, and I was trying to get off.

He didn't give me a warning this time. The belt came down across my ass. I let out one scream, then my body began to shake and I rode the tide of euphoria out.

I collapsed on the bed and gasped, "I can't take it anymore. Please do it."

He grabbed me by the shoulders and kissed me, pushing his tongue into my mouth until I moaned. He pushed me back on the bed and fucked me so hard it knocked the breath right out of me. But I took it and wanted more and I began to come then, so hard, nothing like it I'd ever felt. The orgasm seemed suspended in the air, holding on to me tight, never letting me go. I screamed with it and screamed until it fell away from my body.

He turned me over and put one of my legs up on his shoulder then he put his hard, throbbing cock in me. He began to ride me then and I laid there wanting to move but unable to do anything but pant.

He was now pumping into me. I could tell he was about to come. He fell on top of me, taking my hands and holding them above my head. I began to move with him. We stared into each others eyes as we fucked and we reached that plateau together, nearly fainting in our lust for each other, nearly blacking out as we came together.

As soon as it was over, we didn't say one word. We didn't have to. There was nothing to say.

After that, the blindfold became a regular. This continued for a while, the sex becoming so intense, so powerful that we could do nothing afterwards but gasp for air. A few times, he incorporated a gag into our sex, so I couldn't talk. I mean, so I couldn't beg.

It continued like this until he said those magical words, "Tomorrow I'm going to tie you up."

Stop.

"What?" I asked, staring at the rope in his hands.

"A word," he said. "Any word. A safe word. We need a word. If things go too far, you say the word and I stop."

I felt a wash of relief come over me. I smiled and thought about it. And thought some more. What word? Then I had it.

I stared him in the eye and said, "That's easy. Stop."

He nodded and I could tell he was pleased. I was pleased, too.

"Then let's do it."

He tied me, spread eagle, to the bed. I laid there and smiled at him.

"Remember our word," he said.

I nodded. He checked the knots on the robe to make sure I was secure. I smiled at him.

"With blindfold or without?" he asked, ever so politely.

"With."

He nodded like my answer pleased him, then blindfolded me. Within two seconds, I began to panic. I couldn't move. I couldn't see. I was trapped. I was alone.

He was there. He was there beside me, his hand on my arm, caressing it, caressing me. I willed myself to be strong.

"What would you like me to do?" he asked.

"Anything," I breathed, almost squirming under his hot touch. It was almost as if his hands burned into me. I wondered if they had made a mark.

His hands played with my breasts for a moment, then moved down my belly and into my triangle, then into my cunt. I moaned and tried to raise my hips off the bed. I couldn't. I was tied too tight.

"Ohh," I moaned.

"Shh," he whispered in my ear.

I quieted myself.

His breath was on my neck again, his lips near my ear. He whispered, "I want to put it in your ass."

Uh. Uh?

"Can I do that, Kristine?"

We'd never done that before. I didn't really like anal sex.

"I'm going to put it in your ass," he said.

I said, "Frank, I don't think I want you to."

And then, the switch came out, hitting me across the leg. I trembled but didn't let out a wail. That's how much self control I had.

"I'm going to put it in your ass," he said and he began to untie me.

"What are you doing?" I asked.

"We can't do it like this," he said as he untied me.

He was right.

"Oh."

As soon as he had me untied, I sat up and was told to lie on my stomach. I did as I was told, then he tied me to the bed, spread eagle. I laid there and tried not to cower.

I heard his zipper come down. I tensed as he pushed two pillows under my ass, so it was sticking in the air. He pulled my buttocks apart and his finger slid along my ass, then into it. I tensed. I liked that part. I was just unsure of the other.

I felt a cool liquid on my ass then. Lube. He was lubing me up. I tensed. Then I heard my vibrator start, its soft buzzing floating into my ears like music. I almost smiled.

"We'll start like this," he said. "To get you ready."

"Okay," I sighed.

The vibrator had nothing on the size of his dick. I could handle the vibrator. He'd even put it in there a few times. I sighed as it went in, pushing deep inside me, making me feel whole as it stretched my ass to accommodate its size.

He played with my ass for a little while, getting me ready and by that time, I was more than ready for his dick to go in there. I felt the tip of it at first, then it disappeared, then he gently pushed the rest of it in there, all the way down until I could feel his balls bounce against my ass.

"Ahhh…" I moaned.

"Ahhh…" came his reply.

He began to fuck me then, up the ass. It was so tight, my ass with his dick in there. I tried to move. I couldn't move. I had forgotten I was tied to the bed.

Before he moved again, he took my vibrator and put it next to my clit, turning it on high, just the way I liked. I could have cried my thanks, but all my thoughts were on his dick then, so much a part of me. He began to move, which made me move as he pounded up against me, his balls slapping against my ass as he thrust.

"You are so tight," he moaned. "I've never seen such a tight ass."

My eyebrows shot up involuntarily, but I didn't pursue the thought of whose ass he might be comparing mine to. I couldn't do anything but allow my clit to reach orgasm as he reached his. It was intense, much more intense than I thought it'd be. It was the pain, the ever so slight pain, combined with the joy that made it the way it was: Intense beyond compare.

"Oh, Kristine!" he grunted. "I love fucking your ass!"

"I love you to fuck my ass!" I grunted back and the orgasm intensified. "Fuck my ass harder!"

"I'll fuck your ass harder," he grunted and did just that, but not before giving me a good, hard slap across my ass cheek, which made me shiver and made the orgasm intensify more. It just grew, that orgasm, and I thought it was never going to end. I laid there as he fucked me and it grew and grew and grew and I wailed with it, because of it, taking the corner of the pillow and biting into it to help ease the pain of it and make it last.

"I'm coming," he moaned. "Oh, God, I'm coming!"

I was already there, had been there. I was still getting jolts here and there from it. In a moment, it was gone.

He pulled out of me just as it faded away. I was gasping by that point. Then his mouth was on mine, his tongue probing it open and my tongue in his mouth, where he sucked on it until I fell away from him.

"I love you," he said and gave me little kisses all over my face before removing the blindfold. "I love you so much."

I blinked in the bright light and looked into his eyes. It was true. He did love me. And for some reason, that was scarier than any game we'd ever played. And I was at a loss for words.

He waited on me for seconds, not moving. He waited for me to respond, verify. I did love him, I loved him at that moment. I loved him during sex. And I didn't have a problem admitting it to him, only to myself.

I smiled and said, "I love you, too."

He sighed with relief.

"What's for supper?" I asked, hoping to change the subject. "I'm starving."

Slave to love.

That was the way it was.

He'd tie me up. Or not. If I begged, he'd switch me. Once he tied me to the bedpost and left me. He wanted to see how long I could handle it.

"*FRANK!*" I had screamed thirty minutes into it. "FRANK!"

God, was this going to be like the wine cellar but with no wine and no floor to lie down on? I stood there for a moment considering my options. Well, I could stay here. For a little while, then he'd surely be back.

I decided to do that and I hung from the bed for the longest time. I have no idea how long I was there.

I stood there and stood there and my arms grew heavy and numb. They were asleep. And one of them was itching so bad I was about to start gnawing at it.

I stood there and willed myself to be good.

I stood there and waited for him to come get me.

I stood there and fantasized about beaches and Bourbon Street and a new car.

Hanging there like that made my thoughts torturous. I kept thinking, *He doesn't love me, he doesn't love me. He wouldn't do this if he loved me. He couldn't love me, not and do this to me. He couldn't.*

I sobbed, realizing it was true. It had to be. He would never do this to me if he loved me the way he said he did. I should accept it. I should be on my way. But I was powerless around him. He had me in his orbit and I was spinning out of control.

I stood there and cried. And cried and sobbed and wailed. The crying broke me. It was the crying. I began to cry and feel sorry for myself. I began to feel bad, anxious. And when the crying stopped, I began to scream. I screamed for Frank, for my mother, for God, but especially for him.

And no one answered.

Just before I broke and screamed "STOP!" I thought I couldn't stand it another minute. Not one second longer. I thought I was going crazy. Then he came into the room, walking quickly as if he couldn't get to me quick enough. The rope was untied and he massaged my wrists and arms and kissed my cheek. When I told him how it felt, how it felt that I couldn't move or do anything about it, he chuckled and said, "You've never had any patience."

"It wasn't you hanging there," I said.

He nodded. "Maybe this isn't one of your strongest games, baby."

He was right. We never tried it again.

Happy man.

I have never been so addicted to another person's body before. I craved him. When he was away from me, I ached as though I had lost part of myself. Upon his return, I was whole again.

Everything became about him. About us. I ceased to exist other than for him. We became so close an army couldn't have torn us apart.

We began to talk. We talked so much I can't remember what it was about most of the time. He began to tell me everything about himself, telling me he had inherited everything he had, even his huge real estate business, from his father, who had died when he was very young. He had been raised by aunts.

He never spoke of his mother. I asked him about her once, but all he did was shake his head sadly. I didn't pursue it. When he was ready, he'd tell me.

I told him what I thought he should know, leaving out the boring stuff. The past ceased to matter anymore. I lived in the present, in the now. In our next tryst, knowing it would fill me to the point of exhaustion.

We only had meals I liked. No more frou-frou stuff. Meat and potatoes. Chocolate cake. Soda pop.

We rarely went out, even to eat or shop. The world outside that doorstep didn't matter anymore. All that mattered was when he would be home and what we would do next.

I was obsessed. With him and his body. With his hands and what they did to me.

I loved every single minute of it. I loved knowing he was in control and I didn't have to think about anything. All I had to do was lie there and let the pleasure begin and end. Then the cycle would start all over.

It was natural, a natural progression. I didn't wonder or worry about what was going on or where it was headed. I knew it would eventually end. I took it for what it was and it was our life. And this is the way we lived it. Secluded and sequestered from the entire world. Alone we stood, holding onto each other as tightly as we could. We regretted to fall asleep because that would be time that we were apart. He began to come home earlier everyday. As soon as he could, he was skipping up the walk and into my arms.

And once we were together, once we were alone, nothing else mattered. Nothing else ever would.

Afterwards, he'd give me a bath, or rather, we'd bathe together, giggling like little kids as we soaped each other up. We got so lost in each other during those sessions, I sometimes wondered if it were healthy to be that enamored of another human being. He cleaned my wounds if there were any and he'd feed me off his fork, as I'd feed him off mine.

But I knew my time was almost up. My deadline was nearing. I knew I had to keep it. If I didn't, I was going to be there forever and though I was more than sure I loved him, I knew sooner or later it would be time to move on. I figured sooner was much better than later.

"Frank," I said, staring at him. "Would you do something for me?"

His head jerked up and he smiled, "You know I would do anything for you."

I smiled. Who was the real slave here?

I lied, "I need some money. For my mother. Could you give me some money?"

He nodded and walked over to his desk, pulled out his checkbook and handed it to me. I fingered the thick leather and stared up at him.

"Just write the amount and I'll do the rest," he said, sitting back down. "I can even cash it for you tomorrow on my way home."

Should I? Did I dare? Why not? He tested me all the time. I'd test him. I wrote in a preposterous amount, even becoming embarrassed at it, but he didn't blink an eye and the next day, he brought the money—in fifties and hundreds—to me, delivering it in a bank bag. Delivering it to me with a big smile on his face, as if he were happy to deliver it, glad he could accommodate me.

He bent and kissed my cheek, before turning to leave the room. He called over his shoulder, "I've made dinner reservations. Please be ready in an hour."

I stared after him. It suddenly dawned on me. He was happy. He was a happy man. I'd never really noticed this about him before. Had it always been there? That happiness? He was so happy, he was nearly elated. Had I done that? Had I made him that happy? If so, why wasn't I feeling it too? I discovered the answer to my question about as soon as I asked it. I couldn't feel it because I wouldn't let myself feel it. I didn't want to give it away. I didn't want to lose control, like the way he apparently thought I had. I could fake it, sure, for a little while, but soon he'd catch on. He was too smart not to.

All I had to give him was my body. I knew it then. I knew it and it saddened me. But I couldn't do anything about it but hang on and hope it would change. But can a leopard ever really change its spots? No. And neither could I. No matter how badly I wanted to.

Birthday girl.

Frank decided to throw a big party for my birthday on December 10th. I'd never had anyone do something like that for me. He told me to invite anyone I wanted and he'd invite a few "friends". I didn't know he had any. He never took or made calls from the house. No one ever stopped by. Maybe he communicated with them via email.

I was excited as a teenager on her sweet sixteen. I picked a perfect little black dress, perfect heels, had my hair done. He took care of the rest. The house was decorated with flowers.

I invited all my stripper friends, who I knew would stir up a little trouble. And I invited my old friend, Chelsea, who had been the one to bring me to New Orleans in the first place. She was very excited when I called, but couldn't come. She promised to come down later on. I was disappointed. I really missed her. I was even beginning to miss my little town from time to time. I'd think about the one red-light or the hardware store and I'd get all nostalgic. But I knew I belonged here. I loved New Orleans. I wasn't about to leave.

The morning of my birthday, he woke me up with breakfast in bed. On the tray were two little blue boxes. Inside one box was a pair of platinum and diamond earrings that took my breath away. In the other box a huge diamond and platinum ring. An engagement ring. It looked like an engagement ring. I stared up at him.

"It's a family heirloom," he said and slipped it on my finger.

I waited for him to continue. Was he going to ask me to marry him?

He didn't. He only smiled at me.

"I wanted you to have it," he said softly.

I stared at it. I didn't dare ask, but then I had to. "Isn't this an engagement ring?"

He shook his head. "No. I'd want to give you a much bigger ring than that."

I blinked. Bigger than this?

"I haven't found the right one yet."

The right one? *Yet?* I almost panicked but I pushed the thought of leaving out of my head.

"Thank you," I said. "It's beautiful."

"Not as beautiful as you are."

I smiled and laughed a little. "Come here."

He bent over me and I put my arms around his neck, pulling him down on me and I showed him my appreciation immediately. Jewelry will do that kind of thing.

I scampered around all day, singing *Happy Birthday* to myself and to anyone who would listen. I ate pizza for lunch and washed it down with a beer.

The guests began to arrive around eight. Jackie and two of the other girls I'd worked with (and had partied with at the other party I'd thrown) were the first ones to arrive. When we saw each other, we hugged and jumped up and down. They admired my new earrings and the ring and told me I was one lucky bitch.

I knew I was.

His "friends" were fashionably late. Same look as he had, same reserved manner. They came in with their highly fashionable girl-friends, who hung like starlets from their arms.

One of them told me, "Frank is such a good guy and so sexy! How'd you manage to land him?"

I smiled smugly to myself. If she only knew.

I sighed and said, "Don't you mean, how did he manage to land *me*?"

She threw her blonde head back and gave a fake, high-class laugh. I tried not to cringe.

The party was in full swing by ten. The food and drink flowed. People seemed to be having a really good time. Around midnight, I glanced up at the top of the stairs. Frank was standing, leaning on the railing and staring down at me. I lifted my glass to him. He smiled genuinely at me as though he were more than happy he was able to please me. Then he jerked his head to the side, indicating he wanted me.

My heart began to pound.

I set my glass down and tried not to run up the stairs to him. I took one step at a time, loving the way he looked at me as I neared him. I loved the way he waited patiently until I was on the top step and I loved the way he extended his hand to help me to the top. He encircled my waist with his arm and led me into one of the guest bedrooms.

I nibbled at his ear and whispered, "Thanks for the party."

"You are more than welcome," he said and opened the door.

I went in and he closed the door behind him. I turned and grabbed his head, pulling him into a wet, lusty kiss. He let me kiss him for a moment, then pushed me down on the big, four poster bed.

"Get undressed."

I grinned. He was taking control, as always. I loved it. I loved it when he took control. I was lost in his control and I could let my body do what it wanted to do: Get off.

I sat up and turned, said, "Please help."

He reached over and unzipped my dress, all the way down. I liked the way the zipper sounded, I liked the way the dress fell off my back. I liked the way his eyes devoured my body each new time, as if this

were the first time he'd seen it. I liked that he never tired of it, of my
body. Or of me.

I liked that I didn't tire of him.

"You don't have any underwear on," he said.

I shook my head. "No."

"Why not?"

"I like the feeling of the dress against my body."

He seemed pleased with my answer.

"Keep your heels on."

I did as I was told.

"Get up on your hands and knees."

I did as I was told.

"Spread you legs."

I did as I was told.

He didn't say anything else. He came towards me, tracing an invis-
ible line along the outline of my curves with the tip of his finger. I
shivered in delight. My breathing became sporadic as I tensed in
anticipation. What would it be this time? Rough? Would he grab my
head and pull me back and suck on my neck? Would he glide in gently, taking his time to fill me? Would he let me to play with myself
while he fucked me?

"I want someone to watch us," he said suddenly.

I froze.

"Would you like that?"

He wants someone to watch us?

He leaned over and touched my breast, grazing his finger along
the nipple until I purred.

Then, "Someone is going to watch us, Kristine. He's in the bathroom right now, peeking through the door."

I jerked my head towards the bathroom door, which was indeed
open a slit, the light peering through. I couldn't see anyone.

Then I heard the crack. Of the switch.

My heart began to pound twice as fast. My breathing became labored. I couldn't catch my breath.

Before I could mutter a syllable, the switch came down on my ass with a *CRACK!* I shuddered in misery, in pain, in elation, in desire, in ecstasy. I shuddered with release.

Again, another whack, then his hand rubbing the mark gently then the switch sneaking up my cunt and the tip flirting with my clit. I shivered, shuddered, moaned, shook, shimmied.

He pulled it away, leaned over and placed his hands where the switch had been. I glanced over at the door. Whoever was inside the bathroom had now moved closer to the light and I could see his shadow.

This made me even wetter. Knowing that some man, some stranger was in the doorway, peeking at us, watching what we did, how we did it, how long we took.

He was suddenly in me, bearing down on me, fucking my brains out. The switch was discarded, it was usually only a teaser, something to get me started, to let me know that there was more, lots more, where that came from.

I stared over at the door, at the shadow of the man inside. Who was he? A "friend"? A business acquaintance? A hustler? Someone he picked up on the street for this very purpose?

Then he stopped fucking.

I groaned and tried to put him back in me. He slapped my hands away and told me to close my eyes. I closed my eyes. The scarf was now covering my eyes. I was blindfolded. Protected from the other man's identity, from Frank's face. I was blinded to the world then, blinded from what he was going to do.

I heard scuffling feet. I jerked my head towards the noise. I heard a zipper and I knew. I knew. Yes, yes yes!

The fucking resumed but Frank wasn't the one doing it. He was gone now. No, he wasn't. There was something in my face, his hands, his lips on my mouth, his tongue in my mouth, then mine in his, his mouth sucking on it, sending shivers up and down the entire length of my taunt body. The other man's dick was in my pussy, fucking me. He was a little hairier than Frank. A little larger. His dick was smaller, but nice nonetheless. He didn't move around like Frank moved, either. He kept it in one place, fucking me from behind, holding my ass still as though he wanted to make sure it wouldn't get away.

I almost laughed. If I hadn't been so turned on, I would have.

Then I felt the smooth shaft of Frank's dick. He was rubbing it along my face. I moaned and grabbed for it with my mouth. He allowed me to have it after he teased it along my mouth for a moment. I took it and sucked it, licked it up and down, then nibbled at it, just the way he liked.

He moaned with approval. I wondered if he and the other man were staring at each other as they both took care of business with me, with one woman, whose orifices were being filled by both of them, by both of their throbbing cocks.

Then they switched.

Ah, yeah. Frank was back in me, where he belonged. I sucked on the other man's dick. It was definitely a little smaller than Frank's. Frank began to slap my ass, the way he always did when he did me doggie. He'd slap it, then grab at it, running his hand along it. Then he'd give a thrust—AH! YES! Just like that one!—and slap it again.

The man's dick was shaking in my mouth. He was about to come. He pulled out and covered my face with his hot semen. I licked at it, then at his cock, until he was good and done.

Frank's face was now buried between my legs, sucking at me. And I was coming as I let the other man's dick drop from my mouth. He kept at it, hitting all my hot spots until I squirted away, the orgasm draining all the energy from my body. He put his cock back in and fucked me until he came, until he was dry and couldn't fuck any-more.

I suddenly realized we were alone. The other man was gone.

After he was finished, he said, "Happy birthday, baby."

"Thank you," I said and smiled at him.

He took the blindfold off. I blinked and rubbed my eyes. He smiled at me. I smiled back and pulled him down on me, kissing his face and lips and him. He kissed back and we kissed for minutes, kissed until my legs parted and his cock got hard again. And then he fucked me while I wrapped my legs around him and fucked his orgasm out of his body, fucked him until I came and came and was left without breath.

He rolled off me and gasped once, then resumed his normal breathing. I moved in close to him and rested in the crook of his arm.

"So?" I asked.

"So?"

"Who was he?" I asked, really wanting to know.

"No one special," he replied.

"Oh, Frank, come on! Tell me!"

He eyed me. "No."

I sighed. "Then who?"

"Do you really want to know, Kristine?"

I stared at him and answered the answer I knew he wanted to hear. I said, "No."

"Good."

We left it at that.

End in sight.

This went on for a year. For a year, we lived and played our games to the breaking point. He was always in control of us, of the situation, of me.

As I said, I loved it.

But obsession will wear off. None of us are immune to that. I wanted him with every fiber in my being and I wanted it to continue forever.

One night after we were finished and he was making the bed, I sat there and watched him, wondering if this was the way it was always going to be.

Not that I minded if it were.

But then, I thought about him. He loved being in control so much and I loved surrendering it to him. What would it be like if I were in control of him? Just once?

I decided to test him.

I stood and walked over to him, smiled, pushed him on the bed and sat in his lap. He hugged my middle and kissed my naked shoulder.

"Frank," I said. "Let's try something new."

His eyebrows shot up. He didn't like me saying that. He arranged the games. I was only a player. He was the coach.

"No, listen," I said. "Don't you ever wonder what it would be like to be me?"

"No."

"Come on," I said. "Haven't you ever even considered what it feels like for me, lying there, letting you take control? It feels wonderful. I want you to experience it."

"No."

"Frank—"

"No, Kristine," he said and pushed me out of his lap. "Let's go to bed."

When I woke the next morning, he was gone. He had left a note on his pillow, telling me he would return in a few hours and for me to stay put. It also told me he loved me.

It was Saturday.

I wadded the note up and got out of bed. It felt strange doing that.

Usually, he woke me up so we could shower and get ready together. So I could have breakfast with him and kiss him at the door, wish him a happy day, then do whatever I wanted. And what I wanted was for him to come back soon.

It's funny, but it never felt strange. Until now.

I showered and got ready. I fumbled around looking for the tooth-paste. Where the hell was it? I finally found it inside the medicine cabinet and brushed my teeth. I stared at myself in the mirror and suddenly got that strange feeling I get from time to time. *Who am I?*

I shook it off and suddenly started laughing. Who *was* I? What the hell did it matter? I thought about that and it did seem strange. Not only strange, but also funny as hell! I started to laugh and laugh and I couldn't stop laughing. I had to sit down on the floor as I convulsed with laughter. I laughed until I cried, then I got up laughing, put my clothes on and I left the house, straight out the front door. And I didn't leave a note.

My car was parked in the garage. It hadn't been driven in so long, I was almost afraid it wouldn't start, but it did and I backed it out and got on the street.

I don't know what my intention was. I just wanted to see something different. Some different faces, some different places, something different other than that house, Frank and all the same places we went to. I saw a mother pushing a stroller with a little, bitty baby in it. I smiled and drove to the stop sign at the end of the street, looked both ways, turned left and headed to the Quarter.

It was early, but there were a lot of people out. It was summer and crowded. People were all over the place, walking out in front of my car without looking. I had a sudden urge to return to the house and escape all this chaos, but I had my mind set. There was a little bistro down here where I used to eat my breakfast. They had the best biscuits and gravy. I was dying for them. Frank made them for me but he always got the gravy wrong. It either came out way too thick or way too thin. It was usually inedible.

I drove around for a few minutes until I found a parking space, pulled in, got out, put some money in the meter and walked to the bistro.

It was busy. I found a seat in the back and sat down. A waitress came by asked me what I'd like and I was stunned at myself when I rattled off, "I want two eggs, scrambled, biscuits and gravy, two slices of bacon—extra crisp—and a sweet tea."

I hadn't even hesitated. She didn't seem to notice.

She nodded, "Anything else?"

"Yeah," I said. "Do you have a newspaper?"

"Sure," she and jerked her head towards the bar. "Over there."

I spotted it and rose, grabbed the paper and hid behind it. In no time, I had my tea, then my food. I ate some of the food, but it tasted different. Maybe they had a new cook. I pushed it away and lit a cigarette and stared around the room. Strangers. All these people were strangers. Tourists. Visitors. Where were they going? Where had they come from? And when were they headed home?

Home. Home. I suddenly wanted to go home so badly, I could have jumped out of my skin. I could have run there in no time. I hadn't seen my mother in months. I should call her.

I threw some money on the table and left the bistro. I walked out, deciding to do some shopping or maybe just walk. Be out with people. I needed that.

I walked for a long time, getting lost in the crowd. I didn't get my palm read or my future told. I didn't go into any shops. I didn't buy anything. I just observed what everyone else was doing. It seemed strange to me, in a way. I had forgotten what it was like, doing normal stuff like this, getting excited over a good buy, or squealing with delight at the sight of the horse-drawn carriages that lined the street with their flowers on top of their heads. I always loved those horses.

Maybe I'd ask Frank to buy me a horse. That would be fun. I loved to ride. Maybe he did as well, though he'd never said one way or another.

Would he buy me a horse if I was leaving? Could I take it with me?

I stopped my thoughts. I wasn't leaving. Not yet. No. I couldn't. Could I?

I shook my head and found myself over near Jackson Square, where all the palm readers set up shop. I had just about decided to get my palm read when I heard someone calling my name. I stiffened, thinking it might be Frank, but it wasn't. It was Chad. My neighbor from my life a million years ago.

"Hey! I thought that was you!" he exclaimed and gave me a big hug.

"Hey yourself!" I said and hugged him back.

He pulled away, marveling at me. "I haven't seen you in forever! I thought you'd moved!"

I smiled at him and said, "No. I'm still here."

He nodded. "I was just about to grab a bite to eat. Want to join me?"

"No," I said. "I've already eaten."

"Already?" He glanced at his watch. "It's only eleven."

"What?!" I said and grabbed his arm. It was eleven. I'd been wandering around for three hours! How had I lost track of time?

"Come on," he said. "My treat."

I stared at him. He was so cute. Tall, lanky. Good natured. He lived in the apartment below mine and Jackie's. I was always running in and out of there and he'd always say, "In a hurry much?" which would make me smile. God, I missed him. I missed running around. I missed Jackie.

"How's Jackie?" I asked.

"Didn't you hear?" he said. "She moved to Ft. Lauderdale."

"What?"

He nodded. "Someone told her the strippers there were making twice as much as they do here and she left."

She hadn't even called me. She hadn't said goodbye. I hadn't been around for her to say goodbye. We were so close once and now she was gone, to a new life.

Oh, shit. Shit.

"So, how about it?" he said and wiggled his eyebrows.

"Sure," I said. "Why not?"

We went to a little Greek place and ate gyros.

Chad talked my ear off, asked me a million questions, which I didn't answer, then told me we should go out sometime.

"If you like," he said. "I always meant to ask you out, then you moved and I kicked myself in the ass. I told myself that if I ever saw you again, I'd ask you. So how about it?"

I smiled at him. Something in me made me almost want to accept, but I couldn't, of course. I couldn't because I wasn't a free agent anymore. I had my man and he had me.

A sudden gust of panic set it. It ate at my insides and made me slightly nauseous. I suddenly remembered my deadline. Knowing it was past made me panic. I wanted to jump up and run, get out before it was too late.

Chad was staring at me as I swam inside these thoughts. I shook myself and smiled at him.

"Sorry," I said. "I'm kinda…"

I trailed off. What was I involved in? What kind of relationship was it? Was it the kind that involved a nursery? No. The kind with diamond rings? No. The kind with white wedding cake? No. Then what kind was it? I didn't know and that saddened me. For a moment. Who cares about that kind of stuff anyway? I knew life was no fairy tale and that included knowing weddings and marriages weren't either.

"Oh," he said and squeezed my hand. "When you get tired of him, give me a call."

I smiled at him. "Sure."

"Great," he said happily.

I nodded and stood. "Listen, I have to get going. I have an appointment I need to keep."

"I understand," he said. "Keep in touch, Kristy."

I stared at him. No one ever called me Kristy anymore. Always Kristine.

"Will do," I said.

He stood and gave me a peck on the cheek. I stared into his eyes, wondering if he could see through me. If he knew what was going on. He couldn't. He smiled back at me and told me to be careful.

I didn't go immediately home. I wandered around a little while in the Quarter, then I got in my car and drove around, looking at strip malls, at houses in the suburbs, at things like I was a foreigner and all of this was new to me.

And it was. In a way.

After darkness had fallen, I decided to go home. He was waiting on me. As soon as I pulled into the driveway, he was at my car, opening the door, demanding to know where I was, who I had been with and why I had left.

"I don't want to talk about it," I said and pushed him away.

He watched me disappear into the house. I went straight for the liquor cabinet and poured myself a shot of Jack.

He stopped in the doorway and watched me.

"What's the matter?" he asked quietly.

"Nothing," I said.

"Where did you go?"

"Out."

"Why?"

I poured myself another shot and said, "No reason."

"Kristine," he said. "Just tell me what's wrong."

"What's wrong?" I said and waved the bottle at him, pouring whiskey all over the floor. "What could be wrong, Frank? I have it made here. You do everything for me, give me all I ever wanted and more."

He swallowed hard. "Just tell me."

I stared him dead in the eye and said, "I can't do this anymore."

"Can't do what?"

"Be with you like this. I can't give it to you anymore. I want to and it kills me to say this, but I can't do it anymore."

"What happened?"

I scoffed, "What do you think happened, Frank? I woke up!"

He stared at his shoes. "What do you want?"

"I don't know," I said and started to cry. "But I don't want this anymore."

"What do you want?"

"I don't know, but I don't think you can give it to me."

His head shot up and a dark cloud settled over his face. I wished I hadn't been so honest.

"What's wrong, Kristine?" he said. Now he was concerned.

"I can't do it anymore, Frank," I wailed. "I just can't!"

He stared at the switch on the floor, where he'd dropped it the night before and never retrieved it, then back at me. He looked almost defeated.

"Do you not love me anymore?" he asked quietly.

No, I didn't. I couldn't. I had shut it off. Today. This morning. Time was up. I had all the money I'd wanted from him and it was, simply, time to go. Move on. Away. Run. Run away.

"Of course I love you!" I said, shaking my head.

"Then what?"

"I don't know!"

And I didn't. It was as if the tables were suddenly turned. And I didn't know what to do now. Besides leave and start over. I was good at that, starting over. I liked it. I liked the newness. I didn't like what I had here anymore. It was so comfortable, it suffocated me.

"If you only knew how it felt," I said. "If I could share that with you—"

"No," he said.

"Please," I said. "Just once. Just let me tie you up once."

"No."

"Either do it," I said. "Or I leave."

And I would, my bags were packed. I had packed them before I left that morning. I had stored them in the trunk. I had planned on leaving and now I couldn't. Not until it was finished. And I still didn't want it to be finished, over, done with. But I had to see what he'd do. I wanted to know how far I could push him. I didn't know what I'd do after he had been pushed, but I wanted to see. Pushing him would tell me something which included whether I should stay or whether I should go.

He knew I wasn't bluffing. He knew I would stand my ground on this one. He knew I wouldn't back down. Now it was in his hands. What to do.

"Either give me control or let me leave."

He started to laugh, but stopped himself. He bent down and picked up the switch.

"Follow me," he said.

I followed him.

We went upstairs and into the bedroom where he solemnly and ceremoniously handed me the rope. And the switch. It felt funny in my hands, the rope. I'd never noticed its coarseness before now. The texture was rough, uneven. It scratched my skin.

Frank was staring at me, wondering what I would do next. What was I going to do now that I had the control?

"Please undress."

He complied, watching me out of the corner of his eye. I stared at him, then at the wall. When he was done, I told him to lie down on the bed.

He lay down.

"Spread your legs and grab hold of the post."

He did as he was told.

I walked over and tied him to the bed. He began to squirm. I hated that. It didn't feel like I thought it would feel. It felt affected, put on. Not exciting, not like when he tied me to the bed.

After he was tied, we stared at each other for the longest time. The tables had turned. I was now in control. Neither one of us liked it. But there was no going back.

I lifted the switch and brought it down on his leg. He didn't even flinch. I felt sick. I ran into the bathroom and vomited into the commode. I got up and rinsed my mouth out with water.

I went back out and stared at him, tied to the bed. Seemingly helpless. But he still had it, no matter how tightly I had tied him, he still had me under control. He had only given it to me this one time to make me stay under the false pretense of giving me what I wanted.

And I didn't want it. I didn't want it any more than he wanted me to have it.

I sat down beside him and kissed him, crying as I kissed him, knowing I would miss him so much I'd want to die. I already missed him and I hadn't left yet.

But that was my nature. I don't deny my nature. Not even with him. I pursue something until I get it and once I get it, I'm done.

And so was he. I left him lying on the bed, still tied up. I left with tears in my eyes, with his money in my pocket, with regret in my heart. I left, knowing I would never, ever find anyone like him, but knowing that that was fine. That it would have to be fine.

Run, run, run.

I wasn't running home to my mother. I wasn't running anymore. I didn't have anywhere to go. I had never felt better.

I've never felt worse. I wandered around, driving for endless hours, endless nights, never sleeping, barely eating enough to sustain me. I stayed in cheap hotels just long enough to take a shower and rest then I ran again, running so much I eventually found myself in a circle, circling New Orleans, circling him.

Sometimes, late at night, I could hear him calling me. From far away, I could hear his sweet voice, telling me everything will be fine, good, better than it ever was before. I wanted to run and find that voice, but I didn't. I didn't need it anymore. I wanted it, but that's another matter.

I told myself to stop. To stop loving him. To turn it off. It was over. It had to be over. Nothing ever lasted and this couldn't last either. I had to leave. I had to! I couldn't go back.

Why?

I asked myself that over and over. Why? Why not return to him? Why not? Why was I running in the first place?

I knew why. I was afraid. I was afraid, not of Frank, but of his love. It was terrifying to me. His loving me. I was terrified I couldn't return it. I didn't know if I had it in me to love him as he loved me. I just figured that it couldn't last, the infatuation, the love, the passion.

And if I gave it back, what if he took it away? What would I do then? I'd crumble. That's what I would do. I'd crumble. And I was too strong to crumble. No one had ever gotten the best of me and I didn't want to start that now.

But it was lasting. The love I had for him was lasting. It wasn't going away. It was tormenting me to know what I had left behind. What I had given up.

But I couldn't go back. There was too much there. Too much. It was too much.

A week passed. A lonely, long week. One week. Only one week and I couldn't take it anymore. I told myself to take it, to let it go, but I kept hearing his voice, sometimes coming at me in a dream, telling me to come home to him. That voice broke me. It carried me home to him. It was my saving grace and my prison. That voice, his voice, which was his love, which I needed, which I told myself I didn't need, that I couldn't need. That I ran from, which I was now running back to.

I ran to it, to his voice, so far away and to him. I ran all the way home, crying, hoping, praying he would be waiting. And he was. He was waiting, his arms spread open. He kissed me passionately, chaining me to him and never letting me go. And I never wanted to be let go again. I never wanted to succumb to my doubts or my resolutions. I didn't have to live my life the way everyone else lived theirs. It was my life and I chose to live it with him. I chose it, to be there. It made me happy to be with him. He was mine as much as I was his. Time had done nothing to our passion. It was as if it had stopped for us and once we met again, it resumed.

"I knew you'd come home," he said.

I had a feeling he did. And that's when I realized what it had all been about. Frank hadn't been trying to break my spirit or my back. He'd been trying to break down that wall I had around myself that never let anyone in. He wanted to break down those walls so he could see, so he could tell if I really loved him. He wanted inside that wall because he loved me. And he knew if he broke it down, I'd love him back. He'd beat me that one time because then, that's all he knew to do. He threw me in the wine cellar for the same reason. He was unsure of my love, unsure of me. And it frightened him and he took his fear out on me. He did those things because he really didn't know if I loved him or not. And that's what made him crazy. He was just as afraid of not being loved as I was. The games had been the way for us to find our love and stake our claim to it. He'd only beaten me to the finish line and he knew I'd soon follow, if he could only hang on for a little while longer. He knew me better than I knew myself.

"Don't ever go again, Kristine," he said, cupping my face in his hands, staring deep into my eyes. "If you ever leave again, I won't be able to take it."

Neither would I.

"I love you," he said, kissing me, sucking on me, loving me. "I love you so much."

"I love you, too," I muttered and took his kisses and gave them back.

"Stay with me forever," he said, forcing me to look in his eyes. "Tell me you'll stay forever. Promise me."

"I'll stay forever. I promise."

And I kept my promise. This time he kissed me and I felt it wash all over me and I fully understood what it was all about. The games. The games were not about succumbing to his control, they were about losing it, they were about letting myself go, letting myself run wild like the wild horses run inside of me, letting myself free, freeing myself to the feeling not of ecstasy but of love. The games were about nothing other than love. I knew that now.

And with that realization, I shuddered with release and I let everything go. Nothing mattered. With that final resolution, he broke me. He broke me. No. I broke myself. I broke myself of those chains that never did anything but hold me back in the first place. I loved him.

And I allowed myself to love him the way I wanted to love him, the way I had to. The way I needed to. And I allowed myself to accept his love.

And there was no going back after that, never again would I show any ambivalence on it. I loved him. He loved me. That was all we had and that was enough.

The girl has been broken.

0-595-24057-7

Printed in the United States
697700002B